Printed in the United States of America

Revised Edition, 2022

ISBN: 978-0-9982120-4-3 (print)

ISBN: 978-0-9982120-5-0 (e-book)

Fonts: Yikes!, Garamond, Abadi MT Condensed Light

Visit the author's website at www.martina-fetzer.com.

Cover art by okdoodle.net. Edited by Jessica Nelson.

This is a work of fiction. Names, characters, places, and incidents either are the products of the author's imagination or are used fictitiously. Any resemblance to actual persons, living or dead, businesses, companies, events, or locales is entirely coincidental. Also, the author isn't wealthy enough to make a lawsuit worthwhile.

the Bedazzlers

MARTINA FETZER

CONTENT NOTE

This book is meant to be lighthearted, but it's written for adults and contains content that some readers may find objectionable. Content warnings are available at martina-fetzer.com.

For Jack Kirby and the other greats,
without whom I'd have nothing to parody

PROLOGUE

There are two types of people: those who are ripe for a superhero origin story and those who aren't. Doug Daniels was a frail man with large glasses, slicked-back hair, and an alliterative name. That last fact was about the most interesting thing he had going for him. He lived a normal, boring life and did normal, boring things like going to work and resenting having to go to work. In other words, he was the type of person ripe for a superhero origin story.

Doug's wife Sarah embarrassed him with regularity. Her taste in paintings was bad enough. He had tolerated *Bowl of Fruit*, *Chihuahua*, and *House Near a Creek* for thirteen and a half years, but he wasn't sure he could tolerate her latest request. Upon learning that he was heading to the corner store to pick up a few odds and ends, she had asked what should have been an innocent question, were it not for Doug's insecurities.

"Can you do me a favor?" Sarah asked.

Doug's cheeks flushed. His face burned. He knew what was coming. "Not—"

"Pick up some tampons while you're there," she said.

Doug buried himself in his shoulders.

Four scenarios are widely believed to be the most arduous: speaking at a funeral, speaking at a wedding, firing an employee, and being on the hostage end of a hostage scenario. For a certain subset of men, however, peer-reviewed studies have found that buying tampons outranks all of these. Despite decades of research, no one's sure why publicly demonstrating that he's on intimate terms with a woman is so embarrassing to this sort of man.

"Please," Sarah said.

"Okay. I'll add them to the list."

She kissed his cheek. "Thanks!"

"I'll be back in a few." He hobbled out the door.

Doug would not be back in a few.

As he walked the streets of SoHo, Doug found himself consumed by tampon-induced anguish. So much so that he didn't see Monochrome walking toward him down the other side of the one-way street. Nor did he see the tanker truck stopped at the coming crosswalk, its driver distracted.

Monochrome was the world's first public superhero, if a person who wore a cape covered in advertisements and never seemed to help anyone qualified as a superhero. Having just snagged said cape on a piece of rebar, losing an advertisement in the process, he trudged across the street with the frayed ad in one hand and an elaborate latte in the other. In normal times, losing an ad would have been an inconvenience. With sponsors hard to come by, it was a catastrophe.

Across the street, Doug walked head down, repeating the list to himself. "Tomatoes, pie crust, Bran Flakes, grapefruit, Juicity Juice..." He shuddered. "...tampons."

Monochrome made it across the street and prepared to cross again, toward Doug. Though the traffic light had turned green, the tanker truck lurched only slightly forward.

"Hey, Monochrome!" its driver shouted in a thick, blue collar New Yorker accent.

"Hmm?" As the hero turned to face his heckler, his cape fanned out with panache.

The truck stopped in the middle of the intersection.

"Fuck you, buddy!" the driver shouted.

"Stop listening to the news! I didn't do anything!" Monochrome said. When he was angry or otherwise emotionally compromised, his powers emerged. Accordingly, his hands began to glow. "Damn it..."

The torn advertisement caught fire and turned to ash in his hand. Through a newly melted cup, twenty-two ounces of hot latte splashed his white turtleneck and fell to the ground, spraying all over. The hero clenched his fists and thought calm thoughts in hopes of avoiding another magma incident.

Money. Fame. Adoring fans. Money.

The money and adoring fans had greatly reduced in number since his PR disaster, and Monochrome's fame had turned to infamy in much the same way Mel Gibson's did after all the anti-Semitism and domestic violence. Still, the generic mental pep talk cooled Monochrome's hands for the moment.

The driver continued, "I hope that stain never comes out, you piece of shit."

Doug was almost finished crossing his own crosswalk, oblivious to the scene. "Tomatoes, pie crust, Bran Flakes, grapefruit, Juicity Juice... tampons."

Another truck approached the intersection from Doug's right. Its driver had a few diversions of his own: singing along to "Midtown Boogie" and trying to text his cousin about a free piano. He couldn't play the piano, and he didn't know anyone who could, but free was free, so he steered with his knees. His distracted driving would have been bad enough if the truck hadn't been carrying toxic, flammable chemicals, but it was.

Doug didn't see the other truck in the intersection until too late.

"Oh, shit," he said.

The newly attentive driver slammed the truck's brakes, and there was a shrieking, grinding sound as the two trucks collided. They would have skidded toward Monochrome, but instinct made the superhero shoot them with a blast of magma that exploded one truck and tore the other wide open.

Red and blue chemicals rained down, flooding the street and spraying the air. Doug pulled himself out of his thoughts just in time to be bathed in mysterious, searing substances. Screaming is hard with lips that have been melted together with acid, so no one heard Doug's anguish. He twisted in pain as his hair dissolved, followed shortly after by most of his skin.

Monochrome ran not to Doug, but toward the wrecked vehicle to continue his verbal spat with its driver. The driver pulled himself up and out of his toppled cab, coughing and holding his ribs. It was too late to un-burn his face, but with a free hand, he patted away a bit of fire that had caught on his long, blue goatee. It gave way to a thin wisp of smoke.

"I make magma," said Monochrome, "not rifts in space. Got it?"

The traumatized driver submitted. "Yeah, sure. Okay. Whatever you say, man."

Paramedics pronounced Doug dead on the scene.

1

THE ME IN TEAM

G odwin Zane's third biography—*I'm Grey and That's Okay*—was due to release in a year, and it's worth noting that he was, in fact, grey. Every inch of his skin, from toe to tip, was the color of graphite, and it looked extra grey beneath a head of shoulder-length white hair. That's why he called himself Monochrome, even though it would have made more sense to give himself a codename based on his magma power, something like Volcanaut or Pompain. Until a few months earlier, though, nobody knew he had a superpower.

Born rich, Zane had made himself even richer via a series of stunt films titled *Look at Me!*, in which he escaped precarious situations thanks to vague abilities that he never revealed to the public. The does-he-or-doesn't-he-have-powers question had broad appeal, and with the money earned from the films, he made himself richer still developing consumer electronics. Self-driving cars and Zanephones had shareholders beaming... until the rift incident.

A few months earlier, in summer 2015, a rift in time and space appeared over Lower Manhattan, right above Zane Tower. It had been a run-of-the-mill evil scheme to destroy all mortals so a group of immortals could form their own utopian society. Zane melted the device that generated that rift, saving millions but blanketing the entire eastern seaboard in magma particulate. He was wrongly blamed for the rift. He was rightly blamed for the supercharged ash, which contained whatever gave him magma powers and haphazardly granted thousands of people strange abilities ranging from super strength to laser vision to the ability to communicate with plants.[*]

On the sixty-fifth floor of Zane Tower, Zane sat at the head of a conference table, practicing a speech for what felt like the thousandth time to Abigail Waters, full-time journalist and part-time biographer. She sat across from him in an otherwise empty room as he wrapped up his final rehearsal.

"—and so I've called you here because I want to assemble a group of heroes," Zane said, "to face the threats that I can't face alone."

He had, with Abby's help, written the perfect plea for his would-be teammates.

Her mouth made a pleased smirk. "You've got it, Zane."

Godwin Zane always insisted that people call him God for short, so most referred to him by his last name instead, to spite him. There were plenty of reasons to spite him.

"There are no threats I can't face alone," he complained.

Abby waved her hands in the air. "Don't say *that*."

Zane pressed the intercom button. "Send them in."

The door opened and five people took seats at the conference table. Zane faced away from the visitors, looking instead at an enormous, gold-framed picture of himself and smiling because it made his grey skin look fantastic, a contrast to its oft-splotchy appearance in real life. He liked to spin and reveal himself dramatically mid-conversation, and he braced himself, waiting for the moment. Only when he was certain they'd all seated themselves did he speak.

"A few months ago, our world changed in a way that—"

"I can't hear you," a muffled female voice said. "Could you

---

* They don't say much.

turn around?"

Zane straightened his black turtleneck and blew at his hands in a pre-emptive measure. "Ugh. Fine."

When he spun to face the group, he was immediately un-impressed. He knew two of the people who had joined him: Arturo Brooks, a paranormal detective-cum-cyborg, and Archibald Falcon, the Divine Dimensionmaster. The rest were an assortment of Zane Industries employees who'd vol-unteered to join the team because there were bonuses on the line, and they looked so pathetic that he almost gave up on the endeavor right then and there.

"What's your name?" Zane asked the woman who'd spo-ken. He would have already known, but he'd ignored six sep-arate briefings on the team in favor of doing anything else.

She mumbled through a mask. "Blanche Allister. I work in Accounting."

"What's your *deal*?"

It became apparent why Blanche had been unable to hear Zane and why her voice was muffled: she wore a balaclava and ski goggles. Every inch of her plump accountant body was covered in frumpy winter gear despite it being a brisk fifty degrees outside.

"Well—" Blanche extended the word in a nasal, enthused Minnesotan accent. "It's a heck of a story. You see—"

"You got powers when the rift exploded," Zane said.

Blanche got a stupid look on her face, which no one could see. "Gosh. Yeah. How'd you know?"

"Everybody did," Zane said, bored. "What do you *do*?"

No one ever asked Blanche that, so she bounced a little at the opportunity to talk about herself. "Oh. I'm so pale I blind people. That's why I've got these goggles and whatnot."

"*Awesome*," Zane said, as sarcastically as he could. He fol-lowed that with a quiet "useless" meant only for himself but heard by all. "Anyway, I've called you all here to form a su-perhero team to face the threats I can't tackle alone. Why don't you all just go ahead and introduce yourselves, and then I'll explain."

Abby brought her hand to her forehead. It hadn't taken long for the spiel to go off the rails. After a brief moment evaluating every life choice that had led her to work for Godwin Zane, she pulled out her tablet and began documenting the rest of the meeting. There wasn't much about Zane that hadn't been covered in his last two biographies, and with less than a month to her publisher's deadline, Abby figured focusing on the Bedazzlers could help fill space.

The next person to speak was Jack Cashmere from Legal. He delivered a brief, boring explanation of his role there (it involved three separate uses of the term "delegated management"), then got to the good stuff. "I don't know if it's really a superpower, but... you can see I have bone spines growing out of my body."

Everyone could see that. Jack wore an argyle, zip-up sweater that conveyed the exact opposite of a teardrop tattoo, and the sparse spines that poked through it made him look dingy. They varied in length. Some were tiny bone nubbins that barely penetrated the sweater; others were dangerously sharp six-inch spikes that tattered the fabric around them. On his face, the spines resembled a preteen's facial hair. On his bald head, they appeared to be an ill-advised attempt at a youthful mohawk. It was embarrassing for a man in his mid-forties.

"Can you shoot them out or anything?" Abby asked.

Jack glanced at a sad little wrist spine. "I don't think so..."

"It doesn't matter," Zane said. "You're here because research shows I need a token black guy."

Jack tilted his head in silence. Having come to this meeting knowing what to expect from the billionaire, he wasn't shocked by Zane's behavior. Putting up with it would be well worth the bonus.

Zane added, "That's not racist."

"Pretty sure it is," Abby said.

"It's diversity testing. I'm just giving the people what they want—"

The dashing, suited man sitting next to Jack cut off what could have been an argument. "My name's Arturo Brooks." The only unusual thing about the thirty-something's appearance was that his left eye was brown and his right was a vivid, almost unnatural green. In the business world, he was not a big deal like Zane, but a modest one. "I used to be CEO of the Reticent until—"

Zane made a let's-go gesture and finished his thoughts for him. "He's a cyborg, and his dead husband lives in his head."

"You are the *worst*," Brooks said. He was only there because Zane had promised to build a robot body and extract said husband from his head. He leaned back and glowered.

"How come you're a cyborg?" Blanche asked.

"I died and the Reticent turned me into one."

"Against your will?"

Brooks spoke through gritted teeth. "Yes."

"Which parts of you are person and which parts are machine?" Jack asked.

"I don't know. They didn't exactly give me an instruction manual." Brooks gestured at Zane. "He won't help."

Zane shrugged it off. "I don't have the resources—"

"Your company spent three years researching a collar to help dogs communicate with cats," Brooks snapped.

"—or the desire," Zane finished. "You don't have a saleable problem. There are millions of dogs living with cats. How many cyborgs do you know that need documenting?"

Brooks could only think of one. He fumed in silence.

"Next!" Zane said.

Abby introduced herself. "Abby Waters. Northwestern Journalism, Class of 2009. I'm writing Monochrome's next biography because he, quote, 'wanted a fierce black woman' to do it so it would, quote, 'be in the Oprah book club.' I don't actually have any superpowers, but in exchange for some exclusive interviews, I have to be on his super team."

Brooks commiserated. "That sucks. What are you going to do without pow—"

Abby shifted in her chair, unsure how the cyborg would react. "He made me a suit of armor?"

Brooks's face turned red.

"Allegedly," Abby said. "I haven't seen it yet!"

Brooks stared at Zane. "You had time to do that, but you can't spare a robot body to get Eddie out of my damn head?"

Love you too, his husband said, in his mind. Like Brooks, Edward Smith was a paranormal detective... until he died. A Zane Industries invention, The Afterlife™, kept the dad-bodded blond alive in the cyborg's brain, where he had access to seventy-two Afterlife™ scenarios. He'd been through each of them multiple times and found even *Firefly* Season Two boring at this point. Both he and Brooks felt it was well past time for him to re-enter the real world and its nonprogrammed adventures.

"Let me guess," Brooks said. "You're going to tell me robot bodies are *not saleable* either."

Zane snapped back from some idea that was distracting him. "Hmm. No. They're saleable. They just bore me. Next!"

"Ana Nakamura," a young intern said. Consisting of a tracksuit and ponytail, her ensemble said she was ready for action and adventure. Her sulky demeanor said otherwise. She had a hand laid across Jack's on the table, and she wore a fake smile to cover the pain of bone spines in her palm.

"Wait," Zane said. He was a jerk, but he wasn't a stupid one, and as a teenager he'd gone through a brief weeaboo phase. "Isn't Ana Japanese for hole?"

She lowered her head and spoke in a monotone. "Yes. My parents don't speak Japanese." She changed subjects, but not the tone of her voice. "I think you picked me by mistake, though."

"Why?" Zane asked.

"I don't have a useful ability. Just this." Ana motioned at her tabled hand with her free hand. "I have to touch someone at all times or I'll die."

"That," Zane said, "is the worst superpower I've ever heard of."

"Pretty much," Ana said.

Abby typed up some notes and asked a question. "How do you know you'll die, given that you're not, uh, dead? Surely you haven't been holding someone's hand your entire life."

"No," Ana said. "I was holding someone's hand when I got my powers. We let go, and I couldn't breathe. They touched me again and I could. I've been hanging onto people ever since."

"And you just rely on whoever happens to be around to hold your hand?" Zane asked.

Ana shook her head. "No, I have an assistant, Teresa. She got sick from eating Zane Industries cafeteria food yesterday."

"Is that saleable?" Blanche asked.

"Excuse me?" Zane asked, thinking she meant the food.

"A cure for her power."

Ana perked up, just a little.

Zane put a hand to his protruding chin. "Oh, there's big money in curing terrible powers. But if Zane Industries comes up with the cure, it'll look like I gave people powers on purpose to make money off the cure. That's bad PR."

Ana deflated.

Zane moved on. "Arch, perk things up for me, would you?"

A man who appeared to be in his mid-fifties stood up. His royal blue cape, the only one besides Zane's ad-covered monstrosity in the room, came with an oversized collar and copious gold trim. It covered an excessively Victorian outfit, ascot and all. His voice seemed to echo. "I am Archibald

Falcon, known to many as Doctor Queer, the Divine Dimensionmast—"

There was laughter all around the table.

"Doctor Queer?" Jack wondered.

Doctor Queer lowered his eyebrows. "It means strange or odd... peculiar!"

"Not for, like, forty years, dude."

"I have been alive since 1821! My task is to protect this dimension from rifts, portals, paradoxes, antitheses, and—"

"No offense, but you've kind of been doing a shitty job," Brooks said.

Everyone nodded. In addition to the power-granting 2015 rift, sixteen thousand people had died in the Six Block Disaster of 2014.

"*I'll have you know,*" Doctor Queer said, "that while you were meddling with those petty affairs, I have been protecting the very fabric of reality itself fighting the dread Percival. Were it not for me, billions would have perished!" With his compulsive, flowery hand gestures, he very nearly smacked Blanche.

"Dial it back," Zane said.

"So, what does he have on you?" Abby asked.

Doctor Queer raised an eyebrow. "I beg your pardon?"

"Why are you stuck here with the rest of us? Arturo and I are trying to scam something out of him, and the rest of these poor fools work for Zane Industries. Why are *you* here?"

"Ah," Doctor Queer said. "Godwin and I have been friends for quite some time. He asked if I'd accompany the team, and I agreed."

Everyone shared a silent blink.

"Why?" Abby asked.

"You have friends?" Jack wondered.

Zane scoffed. "Of course I have friends. I used to have a three-thousand-member fan club."

"*Used to,*" Brooks repeated.

"Stop antagonizing me," Zane said. "You're all getting my money."

The group obliged, for the moment, and Zane dismissed their complaints with a wave of his hand. It was time to get to what he alone felt was the most important matter. "So, first things first. Is there anyone in the room who doesn't like Depeche Mode?"

Jack started. "What does that have to do with—"

"I don't know what a Depeche Mode is," Ana said.

Zane's hands began to glow. "Abby?"

Abby let out an overworked sigh. Used to this, she grabbed a nearby fire extinguisher and blasted him with it.

"Thank you," Zane said. All things considered, he was doing a great job controlling his outbursts—both of temper and of magma. He dusted some fire extinguisher residue from his sleeves. "I'll make a note to get her a copy of *Violator*. In the meantime, we need superhero names."

Jack raised his hand. "We haven't even agreed to be on your team—"

"Let's be honest. You're going to," Zane said.

His confidence was convincing. So were the bonus checks. The room shared a collective, resigned shrug.

"Now let's talk codenames," Zane said.

Blanche interrupted. "Wait a tick."

In lieu of sighing, Zane let out a frustrated, "Sigh."

"What's the world need another team for when it's got Defense Squad Z?" Blanche asked.

Zane's hands began to glow, and Abby blasted him with the fire extinguisher again.

A plume of white dust flew into the air as Zane stood and paced. "Defense Squad Z *stole* my idea! They wouldn't even have powers if it weren't for me, and now the government hands them awards for... for what? For putting up flood barricades? They're basically the National Guard. Useless!"

"The National Guard isn't useless—" Abby started.

Zane continued ranting. "The Z doesn't even stand for an-ything!"

"But, like, what are we going to work on that they don't?" Jack asked.

"We're going to stand up for the little guy," Zane said, without explaining how. "We're going to ride a wave of pop-ulism straight to the top!"

The group offered apathetic shrugs.

"Now. Names." Zane's tone demanded focus.

Brooks leaned forward. "Well, I've thought about it, and I'm good with just—"

Hispandroid, Smith said, in his husband's mind.

"—Agent Brooks."

"That's lame," Zane said, "but fine." He looked at Jack. "How about you?"

"I'm gonna go with Cactus Jack," Jack said.

Zane frowned. "No. I don't like it. You're the Human Por-cupine."

"No, I'm not."

"Yes you are."

"No. I'm not."

Zane ignored Jack's last protest and faced Ana. "You?"

"I'm going to call myself Human Touch," she said.

Zane smiled. "Big Springsteen fan?"

"I have no idea who that is," Ana said.

Abby pre-emptively blasted Zane with the extinguisher.

"Thanks for that," he groaned. "And you?"

"Torpedo," Abby said.

"I like it." He looked around the room and recapped. "Monochrome, Torpedo, Doctor Queer, Agent Brooks, Hu-man Porcu... Cactus Jack, and Human Touch. The Bedaz-zlers."

"You forgot me," Blanche said.

"Oh," Zane said. "Um... and Blanche."

"I don't get a superhero name? I was thinking maybe

Lightbringer or—"

Jack interrupted her with an important question for Zane. "Are you married to the team name?"

"*Excuse me*?" Zane asked.

"It doesn't exactly inspire hope," Jack said.

"Or fear," Ana said.

"Or anything at all," Brooks said.

Blanche nodded. "It is kinda dumb."

Zane tapped his fingers and thought pleasant, non-magma thoughts. "When you're the ones worth billions of dollars, you can name your *own* superhero teams after your *own* favorite movies."

"Can we at least talk about why *Bedazzled* is your favorite movie?" Abby asked, her fingers ready to take some notes. "Does it have anything to do with 1994?"

"*No.*"

"I still don't have a superhero name," Blanche whined.

Nobody acknowledged her as Zane moved on to the next subject: their base. The Bedazzlestation, he explained, was located beneath the Upper Bay. His wealthy parents had originally built it as the starting point for a utopian undersea society, but they forgot to pump oxygen in. Everyone died. He'd corrected their mistake and had it converted it into a place where they could practice using their powers without anyone's knowledge.

"It's accessible from the basement of Zane Tower," he said. "Three-factor authentication... high-speed train—"

Everyone was intrigued. Everyone but Brooks, who already knew about the three-factor authentication and was preoccupied with his own mind. Everything in The Afterlife™ felt like reality. While Brooks's body sat at the conference table, he and Smith were wrapped up in the Cozy Sweater scenario, in which the entire world was blanketed in one enormous, cozy sweater. They cuddled together in an extra wrinkled, extra cozy portion. It was warm, like the

Earth-sized sweater had just been through a galaxy-sized dryer.

Stop it, Brooks said.

Nope, Smith said, nibbling his ear.

I need to focus on the briefi—

Smith laughed. *You sure don't.*

In reality, Zane stopped explaining the train setup and frowned. "Brooks, are you even listening?"

"Hmm?" Brooks snapped out of it and let everyone know the reason for his distraction. "Sorry. Eddie..."

"Tell him to knock it off or I'll give him the 'Careless Whisper' again."

"First of all, we share my senses, so he can hear you. Second of all, hang on..."

Brooks switched from speaking out loud to communicating in his mind (i.e., thinking).

The what now? Does that mean what I think it means?

Smith shrugged. *Do you think it means I slept with Monochrome?*

Brooks took that as the confirmation it was, and he pulled away. *You slept with Monochrome?*

Yeah, Smith said, similarly disgusted. It was a long story.[*]

You... Brooks drew each word out like it was the first time he'd ever pronounced it. *Slept... with... Monochrome?*

To be fair, you had broken up with me at the time.

Brooks sank into a low spot in the sweater. *I'm not mad you slept with somebody else. I'm mad that it was Monochrome. Of all the disgusting douchebags...*

Smith tried to smooth things over. *Oh, I agree with you, but that disgusting douchebag is the only reason I'm still here.*

I thought he was straight, anyway, Brooks said.

He is. It was a whole thing.

Okay, but Monochrome, Brooks said.

---

[*] Called *Time Purge*. It's not actually that long.

I know you hate him, but—

If you say "Let's hear what he has to say," I'm kicking you out of my head.

I'm just saying. It might be nice... Smith switched from speech to song. *It might be niiiice—*

Don't do it, Brooks warned.

—to have Monochrome on your side.

In the real world, Zane tapped his watch. "Are you done? Can we continue?"

"No," Brooks griped. "He won't stop quoting *Hamilton* at me."

"Great show," Jack said.

"Mmhmm," Zane said. "Have you seen it? I've been trying to get tickets for months, and even I can't do it—" He had actually bought resale tickets on several occasions, but was barred from the Richard Rodgers Theater thanks to a non-magma incident at *Romeo and Juliet* a few years earlier.

"I haven't seen it," Jack said, "but the soundtrack is incredible."

There were scattered sounds of agreement.

"No. It's not," Brooks said.

"Can we please focus?" Doctor Queer asked. "We have better things to do than discuss musicals."

"No." Zane circled the table and confronted Brooks. "No we cannot. First there's Depeche Mode disrespect and now... you don't like *Hamilton*?"

Brooks sighed. "No."

"Aren't you, in fact, the orphan son of an immigrant?"

"Yeah, so?" Brooks said. "I'm also gay. That doesn't mean I liked *Brokeback Mountain*."

Abby scrunched her face in disgust. "You didn't like *Brokeback Mountain*?"

I've always said your taste is terrible, Smith said.

"It was robbed for Best Picture," Jack said.

Blanche nodded along. "Freakin' *robbed*."

"Right!?" Abby threw up her hands. "It lost to *Crash*."

Ana didn't know what anyone was talking about, and she just nodded along.

Smith, meanwhile, was boasting. *I can't help that my taste is better than yours.*

Your taste? Brooks asked.

Still on the sweater, Smith smiled a smug smile. *Yep.*

Your taste is for banging Monochrome and killing yourself!

The smile disappeared. *Harsh. True, but harsh.* Smith had, after several failed attempts at killing himself, accidentally killed himself, dragging both detectives into this Bedazzlers mess in the first place.

"—To the Bedazzlestation!" Zane said, in the real world.

Brooks had missed quite a bit of conversation. "The what now?"

2

THE BEDAZZLESTATION

T he Bedazzlestation was not as impressive as Godwin Zane believed its name suggested. Sure, it was novel that they had a base under the sea and there was plenty of room for the group to work, but everything was decorated in a 1960s sci-fi aesthetic. Mod women with conical breasts draped in silver fabric would have been perfectly at home between its mint green walls. Worse than the decor, nobody had ever bothered to clear out the bodies of those who died in the sea society's collapse. Hunkered over skeletons inhabited every room, including the Situation Room where the Bedazzlers found themselves as Zane began their grand tour.

"We have cameras all over the world," Zane said, gesturing at a wall of CRT monitors. He made it sound like the cameras belonged to him, but in reality they played a selection of TV news stations and live webcams. Three were dedicated to the Cincinnati Zoo's AntelopeCam.

Ana was not concerned with the monitors as much as the corpses seated across from her. Her voice diverted from its calm monotony. "I'm going to be sick. Nobody said dead people were going to be part of this internship."

She tugged at Jack's spiky hand, and he dutifully followed her to a wastebasket.

"I don't see the big deal," Zane said as the intern vomited.

"Of course you don't," Abby said, shedding her Fakael Kors jacket in the stuffy Bedazzlestation.

"Question!" Zane said.

"Yes?" Doctor Queer asked.

"Is it normal for your biographer to antagonize you?"

Doctor Queer put a hand to his chin and pondered. "I don't have a biographer, as my work must occur within the bounds of secrecy promised—"

"Yeah, it's normal," Brooks said. "So long as the person being antagonized is you."

I love angry you, Smith said. *When I get that robot body, we're gonna need so much WD-40...*

"Question!" Blanche said.

"What are you doing?" Zane asked.

Blanche sank in her chair. "That's not how we announce that we have questions?"

"No. That's my thing, and you can't have it." Zane crossed his arms. "What's the question?"

"Are there any Cthulhus down here?" Blanche asked.

"There's only one Cthulhu," Jack said, "and it's fictional. I hope."

Blanche's face scrunched. "I figure if we're under water, there's gotta be some Cthulhus."

Zane shook his head. "No, Blanche. Not all sea monsters are Cthulhu."

"So there *are* sea monsters?" Brooks asked.

Zane waved his question off.

Abby opened the coat closet and immediately slammed the door shut. She turned to face the group with a blank expression. "There's literally a skeleton in that closet," she said, setting her jacket on a chair.

Zane sighed. "Do you all *really* want the skeletons out?"

"*Yes*," everyone said at once.

"Fine. I thought they added a nice ambience, but fine. But I'll have you know they're so old you could just smack them and turn them into dust." He demonstrated on a nearby body. With a gentle tap, its skull tumbled to the floor and crumbled on impact.

Ana's body tried to puke again but came up with nothing but a few retching sounds.

Brooks eyed the pile of bone dust with suspicion. "When was this place built again?"

"1967," Zane said.

"It hasn't even been fifty years," Brooks said. "How are they so brittle?"

Abby perked up, ready to take notes. "That's a good point, actually."

Zane's eyes shifted. "There... may have been experiments." He waved toward the doorway. "Let's keep this tour moving."

Aside from the Situation Room, there were eight other rooms of note: four bedrooms, a cafeteria, a library, a gym, and a common room to which all the other rooms were connected. Had anyone known of the Bedazzlestation's existence and tried to map it, it would have looked like an asterisk with a bubble at the end of each stick. The group sat around a conference table as their leader attempted to draw something akin to that asterisk on its glass surface with a failing whiteboard marker.

"So the bedrooms—" Zane said, trying to press one last bit of color out.

Jack interrupted. "You know we all have apartments of our own, right?"

"I've got a house on Staten Island," Blanche said.

The room seemed to get a little colder as everyone judged her.

Zane continued. "Anyway. You're all single losers, so it makes sense to stay here so you'll be ready as soon as there's a Bedazzalert."

"I'm not single," Brooks said.

Zane rolled his eyes. "Yes, we're all *very impressed* by your imaginary gay marriage."

Brooks clenched a fist. "It's not imaginary. You officiated it! We have two girls at home—"

Let it go or he'll never get me out of here, Smith said.

Abby was disquieted. "Why did he officiate your wedd—"

"Let it go..." Brooks said.

She scoffed a little and turned back toward Zane. "You said there are four bedrooms. We have to share?"

Zane's voice softened with a PR touch. "If you say it that way, it seems undesirable. You *get* to share. The bonding will be good for the team."

Abby rolled her eyes. "Should I even ask who's roomed together?"

"Take a guess," Zane said.

"I don't know," she said. "I wager I'm either roomed with Jack because we're both black or with Ana because we're both women."

Blanche started, "I'm a wom—"

"The latter," Zane said. "Good call. I'm looking forward to hearing about your slumber parties." His face turned serious. "I mean that. I expect a sleepover report."

The women exchanged angry glares.

"All yours," Jack said, handing Ana off to Abby.

The intern smiled, happy to let go of a man whose hand was covered in spines. Abby grabbed a packet of tissues from her bag and stuffed them into Ana's bleeding palm.

Zane addressed Brooks. "You're with Arch."

"Why?" Brooks asked. Then it hit him. "No."

"Because—"

"Don't say it."

Zane said it. "—Because you're both queer."

"*Maldita sea,*" Brooks muttered as Doctor Queer patted him on the back.

"Guess I get you, Blanche," Jack said.

"This is gonna be super!" Blanche said. "I'm gonna make the place so homey you're just gonna love it. I've got a quilt from Minnetonka—"

Zane faked a cough to interrupt. "Don't you want to know why?"

"Not really, dude," Jack said.

"Sure." Blanche nodded with wide eyes. "Why?"

Monochrome tugged at his cape. "Black and white are monochromatic. It's an ode to me."

Jack gave a relieved chuckle. "That's actually one of the less troubling things you've said so far."

Abby looked at Zane. "I assume *you* get your own room."

"Of course I do," Zane said, as if it shouldn't have been a question. "Not that I'm going to stay here when I have a penthouse."

"But you expect us to stay," Jack said.

Bedazzlers exchanged looks and muttered under their breath. Anger and annoyance were filling the room.

Doctor Queer stood and motioned for the door.

"Godwin, a word?"

Zane followed him out into the hallway.

"What?" he asked.

"I'm aware it's been a rough few months—"

Rough didn't begin to describe the fallout from being blamed for a power-granting rift.

"Yeah, you think?" Zane snapped. "This is it for me. Zane Industries is"—he pressed his fingers together—"this close to going under."

"Yes, well. Given that, you might show more respect to those you've hired to help," Doctor Queer said.

"I am perfectly respectful! Look at the free food and the rooms and—"

Doctor Queer rubbed his forehead. "I understand what you're saying, but you've always had difficulty... hmm... how do I say this?"

"What?" Zane asked.

"You're a tad brazen."

"A tad—"

"A smidge."

"*I know what a tad is*," Zane said.

"Try thinking like a normal human being for once."

"...Said the magician in the shimmering cape."

The doctor frowned.

"*Fine*," Zane said. "I'll try."

He didn't see what was so great about being normal, but when he re-entered the room, he threw his hands out with cheer. "Who wants to talk costumes? I texted some notes over to the Aesthetics Team, and they should be ready any second—"

"I still want to talk about getting rid of the skeletons," Jack said, eyeing one that lay slumped two chairs down the table from him.

"We'll get there." Zane gestured at the door. "Follow me."

They toured the cafeteria, which looked like a cafeteria, and the library, which looked like a library. The next stop, the gym, looked like a gym but held a surprise. Hanging from a clothesline were four costumes, perfectly tailored.

"Are those—" Ana started.

Zane confirmed. "Costumes."

"When did you take our measurements?" Jack asked.

"It was one of the questions in your job application. Don't you remember?"

No one could remember the entirety of the fourteen-page application to work at Zane Industries, only that there had been a long essay portion about Depeche Mode.

"I never applied to work for you," Abby said.

The room got quiet.

"I assume this is mine," Jack said, walking up to one of the costumes. It was a black unitard with a white porcupine silhouette on the chest. Over that lay a black and green varsity jacket. On the ground beneath, a pair of green boots.

"Do you like it?" Zane asked, trying to be normal.

"I told you I'm not going to be the Human Porcupine."

"I was hoping you'd see it and change your mind, but if you *insist,* we can tweak it to be a cactus. The Zane Industries 3D printing lab cranked these babies out in under an hour."

Brooks had already approached what he correctly guessed to be his costume.

"I'm not wearing this," he said.

It was nothing more than a poncho. A multi-colored, striped poncho. With frill.

"I was trying to be respectful of your culture," Zane said.

"I was born *on Staten Island,*" Brooks said.

Blanche tried to give him a high five, but—like everyone— he hated Staten Island and dodged it.

"Well you can't just wear a suit," Zane said. "Diversity test-ing—"

Doctor Queer coughed a little to get Zane's attention, then shot him a condemning glance.

"Fine," Zane said. "Just wear a suit. See if I care."

Ana, in contrast, was quite taken with her costume: a white, sleeveless leotard with a white skirt held up by a red belt. Paired with white, high-heeled ankle boots, the outfit ex-posed the perfect amount of skin to keep her alive while keeping her dignity intact. Since she was only an intern, she wasn't going to bring up the one problem she had with it.

Abby did, on her new roommate's behalf. "A rising sun? Really?" It was on the costume's chest, in bold red.

"I was trying to be respectful of her culture," Zane said.

"I was born *in Queens,*" Ana said.

"Fine, fine. We can rework it into a hand or something to go with the Human Touch name."

"Can we rework this?" Abby asked, eyeing her armored suit for the first time.

"You don't like purple? I thought it was your favorite color," Zane said.

"It's not the purple I'm concerned with so much as the

boob armor." In addition to being overly form-fitting, the suit's power source circled the breasts and lit them with a teal glow.

Brooks squinted at the armor. "That... is radioactive." His HUD said so, plain as day.

"Yes it is," Zane said. "It's powered by Zanium. Completely harmless, low-level stuff."

"How do I fight crime in it?" Abby asked.

"It shoots Zanium rays."

Abby frowned. "Do we get health insurance?"

"All employees of Zane Industries do. Unfortunately, you're working for a bribe, so no. It's fine, though. Trust me."

Abby did not. She began a mental count of how much money she would need to make from the Zane biography to make this endeavor worthwhile. The number was significant, but so was her talent. She decided to press on. "Should I ask why it has a metal faceplate, not a helmet?"

"So people can see your hair and know you're black. Again, diversity. It's basic PR."

The Bedazzlers shook their heads.

Abby held the faceplate to her face and muttered into it, at no one in particular. "It just gets worse and worse." The faceplate amplified her voice, and the words came out booming and robotized.

Zane ignored her and spoke to Doctor Queer. "I assumed you'd keep wearing whatever that is."

"Indeed," the doctor said, pulling his cape tight to his chest.

"And I'll keep on wearing this bad boy," Zane said, pointing at his own becaped outfit. His costume, as it were, was simply his ad-adorned cape over whatever he would normally wear. "So this is the gym, where you can practice using your powers. It's reinforced with—"

"Where's my costume?" Blanche asked.

"...Oh. That must be... a mistake. I'll call and ask about that later." Zane pulled out his Zanephone and left himself a calendar alert to order Blanche a costume. "So, anyway. It would take the equivalent of a nuclear blast to destroy this gym. My magma can't even bust a hole in it. There are practice targets, exercise equipment..."

"A dead guy in basketball shorts," Brooks muttered under his breath.

Zane glowered. "I have some business to—"

"Can I get a mask?" Ana asked.

"Sigh," Zane said. "What?"

"I can't speak for everyone, but I wanted to keep my identity secret."

"I have spikes," Jack said. "I can't hide who I am."

"I possess no civilian identity," Doctor Queer said.

"I've got a faceplate," Abby said, tapping at it.

Blanche shrugged. "I'm covered."

Brooks copied her shrug. "People already associate me with weird rifts and shit. What could we possibly get tangled up in that's any worse?"

That's a jinx if I've ever heard one, Smith said.

Zane scowled at Ana. "You're welcome to provide a mask for yourself. These costumes are visually perfect, as verified by the Zane Industries Aesthetics Department. I will *not* be held responsible for alterations."

Doctor Queer cleared his throat. "It's a fair request."

Zane pulled out his wallet. "Fine. Here's ten dollars, and you can get one from a party store or wherever."

"Thanks." Ana took the money, feigned gratefulness, and resolved to get a mask that completely clashed with her outfit.

Zane moved toward the exit.

"Where are you going?" Abby asked.

"I have a business to run."

"Into the ground," Brooks whispered to Jack, who

snickered.

"I heard that," Zane said on his way out the door.

Abby found herself torn between following him and staying with the Bedazzlers, but she opted for the non-Zane group. As he left, she raised a middle finger at him.

"Bet he didn't hear that," she said.

3

PRACTICE MAKES MEDIOCRITY

Zane hadn't lied about the cleanup crew. As the Bedaz-zlers changed into their costumes for the first time, the Zane Industries custodial staff hoisted decayed bodies into industrial laundry carts. Pieces kept crumbling, but the staff—armed with brooms and dustbins—performed admi-rably. In no time, the gym was cleared of skeletons, and that's where the team stayed.

"You sure you don't mind my wearing the poncho?" Blanche asked, shimmying it over her winter attire. She should have been overheated, but her Minnesotan blood had numbed her to all effects of extreme temperatures.

"Be my guest," Brooks said.

Hey, Smith said. *Psst.*

"Not now," Brooks said.

Blanche pulled the poncho away from her chest and eyed it. "So... I shouldn't wear it?"

Brooks sighed. "I didn't mean to say that out loud. I was talking to Eddie."

"That seems annoying," Jack said.

Abby agreed. "Yeah, can we backtrack to what happened there?" She had her tablet ready to record the conversation. While Zane was her prime subject, Brooks had earned him-self a small amount of fame following a televised vampire-staking incident. That alone made him worth interviewing, and his cyborghood was a bonus.

Brooks dashed her hopes. "I'd rather we didn't."

Ana had a question of her own. "Can you keep your thoughts to yourself, or does he hear everything?"

"How'd he die?" Blanche asked.

"He... I..." The cyborg was prone to existential panic, and the barrage of questions wasn't helping.

Doctor Queer redirected the conversation. "Let's take advantage of the facility, shall we?"

"Yeah, sure," Jack said.

Brooks exhaled in relief.

"Godwin has allowed me to practice here before," Doctor Queer said. He strolled across the room to a janky old computer station and pressed a few buttons. A loud WRRRRP noise announced the movement of a ceiling-mounted conveyer, and soon a gallery of cardboard foes moved across the ceiling, ready to be obliterated.

Ana's mouth went wide, though it emitted the same monotone voice. "Are those supposed to be the bad guys?"

It was a question worth asking. The figures were an assortment of clowns, ringwraiths, and Tom Hankses. As the conveyor creaked, they continued to pass by. The clowns and ringwraiths were repeats of the same picture (from *Bozo the Clown* and *Lord of the Rings*, respectively), but the Tom Hankses ranged from *Turner and Hooch* Tom Hanks to *Saving Private Ryan* Tom Hanks to *Castaway* Tom Hanks, with every Tom Hanks in between.

"I can't shoot Tom Hanks," Abby complained.

Blanche shook her head. "Who could? The man's a national treasure."

"I wouldn't go that far," Brooks cautioned. "He's an average actor."

You're a monster, Smith chastised.

"Did you ever see *Philadelphia*?" Jack asked.

Brooks glared. "Yes."

"That didn't do anything for you?" Abby asked.

"It was fine," Brooks said.

"*Fine?*" Jack asked. "Man, you really do have the worst taste."

"Yeah," Brooks said. "You should see my taste in men."

Hey! Smith said.

The group chuckled.

"So, who's going to kill Tom Hanks first?" Abby asked.

"I'll go first," Doctor Queer said. "I shall aim for a clown, but I make no promises."

He took a rather dramatic fighting stance. With his body facing the clown at an angle, his right arm curled behind him and over his head. His left arm folded in at his side. Both hands were in the awkward position of crossing the pointer and middle finger, folding the ring finger, and leaving the pinkie jutted straight out. He held his chin high, stared at the passing clown, and focused.

"*Ignis Furoris!*" he shouted.

As he fell to his knees in agony, two impressive green fireballs shot from his hands. They sped across the room and hit Bozo square in his cardboard chest. Ablaze, the clown fell to the floor. Abby—still holding Ana's hand—tugged the intern toward a fire extinguisher, grabbed it, and extinguished the magical flames.

"Gosh. You okay?" Blanche asked.

The doctor remained on his knees, cringing. A "yes" barely escaped from between his teeth.

"Do you need help getting up?" Brooks asked.

"No, no." The doctor stood up and awkwardly crossed his legs.

Jack squinted at him. "What was that about?"

"Magic always has a price," Doctor Queer said, shuffling his legs together.

"What do you mean?" Ana asked.

"I thought that was self-explanatory," Doctor Queer said, annoyed. "If magic had no cost, nothing would stop me from using it with abandon. The pain or sheer embarrassment caused by using some of my abilities ensures that I use them only for purposes of good."

Jack still wasn't clear on the explanation. "So you shoot fireballs and—"

"Catch gonorrhea," the doctor said. "It will subside."

"*Oh my God*," Brooks said.

"I chose that spell because its effect is minor," Doctor Queer said. "I sincerely hope you never have to witness my most powerful magic."

Not wanting to think about the doctor's STD, Abby changed topics. "Who wants to go next?"

"I don't have any powers," Brooks said. "I have a HUD and above-average strength. So when we go to battle, I'll just punch stuff, I guess."

"I don't even have the strength," Jack said. "I'm going to have to scratch people."

"Blanche?" Abby asked.

"Gosh. The only thing I can do is blind people, and cardboard won't go blind, so—"

"No point in practicing for you either," Abby said. "Fine. I'll do it."

She handed Ana off to Brooks and placed her hand inside a gauntlet to complete her armored suit. There were no instructions for using the armor, but it did have a pink Zanephone embedded in the hip. She summoned its voice recognition personal assistant.

"Hey, Hot Stuff," she said.

The phone emitted a friendly chime, and a sultry female voice spoke. "What do you need?"

Abby scowled at the phone and raised both hands out in front of her body. "Fire... Zanium rays?"

A teal beam jolted from each palm, and *Captain Phillips* Tom Hanks fell to the floor—his all-American smile blown out, replaced by a hole in cardboard.

She hung her head in shame. "I was aiming for the clown."

"Not bad," Jack said. "Maybe he could just give all of us armored suits. We'd be more effective."

"You know he won't," Brooks said.

Jack sighed. "Yeah."

"Hey, Hot Stuff," Abby said.

"What do you need?" Hot Stuff asked.

"Activate... flight?"

"Flight boots activated," Hot Stuff said.

With that, Abby hovered three feet above the ground. She maneuvered her extended arms for a moment, trying to keep her balance. The suit was intuitive, and once she got a feel for things, she flew around in a little circle.

"Awesome," she said. "I'm not trying to brag, but I think I got the best powers."

"Yeah, almost makes the radiation poisoning worth it," Brooks said.

Abby landed herself with a THUD. "Thank you, killjoy."

"You probably got the best powers because he wants to sleep with you," Jack said.

Abby scrunched her face in silent disgust.

In Brooks's mind, his husband groaned.

Oh, I have some words about that for you later, Brooks said.

Ana addressed the group. "You think they're done with the skeletons yet?"

Doctor Queer pushed the door open. The echoing sounds of backup indicators and workers shouting in Spanish signaled that the crew was not done loading the skeletons, so the group seated itself on a small set of bleachers. Brooks handed Ana back to Abby.

They sat in silence until Blanche blurted, "What's everyone gonna do with their money?"

It was a personal question that nobody wanted to answer, and they sat around failing to answer it for a moment. Stray throat clearings and swallowing sounds were the only response.

Finally, Abby broke the silence with an optimistic answer. "Well, after I make millions on Zane's biography, I'll be able to pursue my passion projects."

"Such as?" Jack asked.

"Shifter erotica," she said, surprised at herself for coming out and saying it.

Her present company did not judge.

"If you need reference material, I'm able to produce shapeshifting spells," Doctor Queer said.

"Yeah, and I know a shapeshifter who owes me a favor," Brooks added.

He actually owes me the favor, Smith said.

"Wow, really?" Abby said. "I'm not going to lie, I was expecting jokes."

Jack plucked a loose spine from the back of his hand and flicked it onto the ground. "It's not the weirdest thing going on around here."

"What about you?" Blanche asked.

"Me?" Jack asked.

She nodded.

"I'm gonna set my mom up in Oakridge Oaks." It was one of the finest senior care facilities in the country, and everyone knew it. There were 24/7 personal aides, pools inside the pools, and hourly sessions of three-dimensional BINGO.

"That's sweet," Abby said.

"Well, she deserves it," Jack said.

Everyone turned toward Doctor Queer.

"As I said, I'm doing this as a personal favor to Godwin," Doctor Queer said. "I have no need for compensation."

Brooks agreed. "Yeah, I'm not getting any either. Assuming the robot body thing works out, I just want to..."

"What?" Jack asked.

"I just want Eddie and I to do regular stuff like eat breakfast or build an Ikea shelf. I've been trying to have a normal life forever, and it... hasn't worked out great so far."

It's working okay, Smith said.

It's really not.

"What about you?" Blanche asked the intern.

"I'm not being paid," Ana said. "The experience should look good on my resume, though."

Everyone made mumbling, consolatory sounds.

"What are you majoring in?" Jack asked. "That being a superhero is a good internship?"

"Criminal justice," Ana said.

Abby raised an eyebrow. "That's actually... surprisingly relevant."

Ana nodded. "So long as we don't break any laws—"

"All clear!" shouted a voice from the common area. The loud THUNK of the seatrain doors closing indicated that the Bedazzlestation was skeleton-free.

"I guess we can check out the bedrooms now," Jack said.

Blanche curled her lip. "Isn't anyone gonna ask about my plans?"

Nobody had planned to, but Abby obliged. "What are your plans?"

"Sweaters for cats." Blanche grinned. "I'm gonna have the biggest cat sweater shop in the country."

"That's nice," Ana lied.

"Mmhmm," Doctor Queer mumbled.

Nobody cared enough about Blanche to tell her the idea was a stupid one.

4

EVERYBODY SLEEPS

The bedrooms in the Bedazzlestation were huge, as each had originally been a dorm room for up to twelve undersea citizens. Despite the space between them, Doctor Queer did not enjoy sharing a bedroom with Brooks. During their first night in the Bedazzlestation's chilliest room, the cyborg had blurted nonsense at no one on six separate occasions. It wasn't a problem in the sense that it interrupted the doctor's sleep—he didn't sleep—but in that it distracted him from practicing the arcane. It was four in the morning on this occasion, and Doctor Queer sat cross-legged and motionless on his bed, emitting a soft purple glow.

"You're not listening to me," Brooks said.

The agitated doctor rolled his eyes, sighed, and resumed meditating.

You're talking out loud again, Smith said.

In Brooks's mind, he and Smith were partaking in the Desert Oasis scenario. It was warm, as deserts tend to be, and they sat at the water's edge, watching it fail to ripple.

Do you have any idea how hard this is? Brooks asked. *Trying to carry on a conversation here and in the real world at the same time?*

You're not talking to anyone in the real world, though, Smith said.

That's not the point. Brooks leaned into Smith's shoulder. *I'm exhausted.*

I know. Smith paused. *If you want, I can exhaust you some more?*

"You're infuriating."

"I'm sorry?" Doctor Queer asked.

"That wasn't for you." Brooks shook his head. "I'm losing it over here."

"Yes, well... staying up past four in the morning probably doesn't help."

"What are you, a doctor?"

Doctor Queer chuckled. "Strictly speaking? No. I was an apothecary before I found my calling."

"And how did you do that?" Brooks asked. He'd been searching for his calling since the Reticent fired him, and he had doubts that living in an undersea lair with a cloaked mage was it.

"Should I turn a light on?" Doctor Queer asked.

"No, I have night vision," Brooks said. "Thanks."

"Hmm... well..." The doctor's glow turned from purple to yellow as he expositioned. "When I was twenty-three, my wife Ambrosia died giving birth to our daughter, Jane. I was distraught and turned to the black arts in an attempt to reach her."

"Did you?" Brooks asked, a little too eager to discuss reaching the deceased.

"In a sense," Doctor Queer said. "It wasn't pretty."

"Sorry," Brooks said.

"Don't be. All happens as it must."

Brooks shot him a disgusted look. "You're kidding, right?"

"I'm not," Doctor Queer said.

"My family was murdered by monsters, I got turned into a cyborg against my will, and my dead husband lives in my head!"

"You're exactly where you should be," Doctor Queer said.

Brooks gave a scornful snort.

"And my family are exactly where they should be."

That seemed grim, and a grim question came to the front of Brooks's mind. "Did you love your daughter?"

"Of course. Why—"

"My mom died giving birth to me and my sister. It's just something I always..."

"You could try asking your father," Doctor Queer said. "You'd get a more definitive answer."

"Murdered by monsters, remember?" Brooks said.

"Oh. I'm sorry," Doctor Queer said. "There was no blame in my case, and unlikely in yours. Still, I progressed down a dark path. It wasn't until I raised the demon Moloch and nearly destroyed Arkansas that I realized I was in over my head."

"Nobody would have missed Arkansas... but I've seen you do magic. If the cost of creating a fireball is getting gonorrhea, how big is the price for summoning a demon or raising the dead?" Brooks asked.

"Nothing."

Brooks blinked. "What?"

"The blackest magic has no cost," Doctor Queer said. "Evil is a much easier path. If I wanted to raise my wife and daughter from the grave, I could do so right now. I know it's not the correct course, though."

"You have the restraint of a saint."

Ha! You rhymed, Smith said.

Brooks clenched his fists. "Teach me?"

"Magic?" Doctor Queer offered a soft laugh. "I don't do that. Each person's journey into the mystic arts is their own."

"Not what I meant," Brooks said. "I mean... you've been alive for nearly two hundred years and fought demons and closed portals and you're just... matter-of-fact about it. A few things don't go according to plan, and I'm losing my mind over here."

"Ah, yes," Doctor Queer said. "Well, it's been a long journey to serenity. I've actually tried to help Godwin with the same thing, and we came up with what he calls the Q.U.E.E.R. Method."

"The queer method?" Brooks asked.

You shouldn't have any trouble with that, Smith said.

Brooks buried his head in his hands.

"Sleep," Doctor Queer said. "We'll discuss it some time when you're better rested."

In the next bedroom over, Jack and Blanche slept peacefully in the caring warmth of Minnetonkan quilts. Both of their dreams centered on sweaters. He dreamt of being bone spine free and no longer damaging his wardrobe, and she dreamt of a clowder of cats, each in a homemade sweater. Neither noticed that the other was snoring.

In the next bedroom over from that, Abby and Ana were wide awake. For one thing, Blanche and Jack's snoring carried through the Bedazzlestation ventilation. For another, during the team's brief recess to gather personal effects, neither one thought to pack any blankets. Those were both smaller problems. The bigger problem was the worst superpower in the world. Even while sleeping, Ana's ability remained the same, and since her assistant was still sick with salmonella poisoning, she clutched her roommate's hand. This made it impossible for Abby—a tosser and turner—to toss and turn. This, in turn, made her toss her pillow in frustration.

"I'm never getting any sleep," she whimpered.

"Sorry," Ana said. "I really do have an assistant for this."

"I believe you. I'm just wondering... does the person you touch have to be... alive?"

Ana gasped. "You don't think I should carry a corpse

around all day?"

"Not a corpse, no. But what if you received a small skin graft? Would that work?"

Ana made a face at the idea. "I don't know. I was really hoping Mr. Zane would research my powers."

"I wouldn't hold my breath waiting for that," Abby said.

"Have you known him long?" Ana asked.

"Not really. Just the six months I've been working on his biography."

Ana posed another question. "Do you think he's as bad as he seems?"

"Does it matter?" Abby asked in return. "He could be the most sensitive person on Earth inside and it wouldn't change anything. People are what they do. They're how they behave. He behaves like an asshole, so..."

"I don't know if that's true, generally speaking," Ana said.

"Well, what do you judge people by?" Abby asked.

"Hard to say," Ana said. "I just get a feeling about them."

"Just a feeling?"

"Yeah."

"If I got that, I might be a better journalist than I am." Abby paused. "I didn't mean that. I'm great at journalism." She was, and she wasn't sure where the doubt came from.

Ana had a feeling about where it came from. "It's not what you want to do."

"No. It's not. Not even a little, but it's the closest thing to writing stories I can do and get paid." She changed subjects. "Do you get a weird feeling about anyone on the team?"

"Weird? No. They all seem okay. You know, other than Monochrome..."

"Even Blanche?" Abby asked, serious. "Someone that into knitting and cats has to secretly be a serial killer or something."

Ana chuckled. "I don't think so. I have an idea, though. You go ahead and sleep. I'll stay awake and move if you move."

"You sure?"

"It's not a problem," Ana said. "I'm twenty-one. I don't need sleep."

"I don't think that's accurate," Abby said.

"It's fine," Ana said.

Abby had a strange feeling of her own, but it could wait. She nestled into the pillow and let her arm hang off the side of the bed for easy grabbing.

Just as she slipped into unconsciousness (some time around five o'clock), Zane's voice echoed throughout the Bedazzlestation: "This is an alert. This is a bedazzalert. Get your lazy asses to the Situation Room."

Abby shot up and sighed, and Ana rushed to grab the arm she'd jerked away.

The alarm repeated: "This is an alert. This is a bedazzalert. Get your lazy asses to the Situation Room."

"That's the alert?" Jack asked, rubbing his eyes.

"Rise and shine!" Blanche said. She was already awake and sipping herbal tea.

Jack groaned. "You know, when I lived in Ohio there'd be these tornado warnings once or twice a month. The siren was right outside my bedroom, and it was loud as hell."

"That so?" Blanche asked.

"This is an alert. This is a bedazzalert. Get your lazy asses to the Situation Room."

Jack cringed. "Oh, it was horrible. But right now? I'd rather hear that." Nearly anything would be better than Godwin Zane's smarmy, condescending voice yelling at them first thing in the morning.

Jack and Blanche suited up and headed to the Situation Room, where Doctor Queer and Brooks had already gathered. There, the smarmy, condescending voice spoke to them in person.

"I hope you all got a good night's sleep," Zane said.

Brooks groaned, making it clear he had not.

"Sure did!" Blanche chirped.

"I didn't," Zane said. "I was up all night with a few *Zanegirl* models, if you know what I mean."

No he wasn't, Smith said. *If he sleeps with anyone, he accidentally magmatizes them.*

Brooks was unsettled. *That's not a word, and I have some serious questions...*

Let me pre-emptively answer them, Smith said. *Yes, he magmatized me. Yes, I was immortal at the time, so it was fine. And about two minutes.*

"Brooks, are you paying attention?" Zane asked.

"No," Brooks said. "I figured you'd take two minutes to get to the point."

In his mind, Smith cackled.

Zane crossed his arms. "Where are the women?"

Blanche frowned. "I'm a woma—"

As she spoke, Abby and Ana rushed into the room.

"Sorry," Ana said, though her voice didn't seem to mean it.

"What's the mission?" Abby asked. She handed Ana to Brooks so she could don a metal glove.

"What took you so long?" Zane asked.

"She has to hold someone's hand *at all times*," Abby said. "Did you not catch that?"

"Does that mean what I think it—" He cut himself off. "What the hell is *that*?"

Ana raised a domino mask to her face and shimmied it into place. "What?"

"You can't wear that," Zane said.

"You told me to buy a mask," Ana said. "So I did."

It was rainbow-colored and adorned with faux gemstones, but those weren't the most appalling part to Zane.

"It's shaped like a butterfly," he said.

"I think it's nice," Jack said.

Zane scoffed. "You would."

"Godwin," Doctor Queer chastised.

"Fine. It's fine. Whatever. Look like an embarrassment. See if I care." Zane tapped a button on his phone, and the monitors behind him switched to display half a dozen news channels, each airing a variant of the same story.

LIVE: MONSTER ATTACKS GROCERY STORE
MONSTER AT THE MARKET
BREAKING: GROCER UNDER SIEGE
LA BODEGA LÓBREGA
MERCHANT OF MENACE
LIVE: TERRORISM IN NYC, OBAMA TO BLAME?

The footage—quick cut and blurry—seemed to show an enormous, purple creature turning over shelves and kicking up floor tiles. It tipped a crate of cantaloupes, sending the melons tumbling. If it were just the cantaloupes, no one would have been upset. But the creature soon moved toward a crate of avocados. There were vivacious screams in the background audio as the monster destroyed the precious life-blood of white hipsters everywhere.

Jack's jaw dropped. "Dude."

"We gotta get over there," Blanche said.

Zane turned to his only friend. "Arch?"

"I'd rather not," Doctor Queer said.

"We need to get to Queens ASAP. You can teleport us. Come on."

The doctor sighed and made circling motions with his hands, enveloping the Bedazzlers in a soft pink glow. "*Movens non moveatur*," he said.

5

BATTLING IS HALF THE BATTLE

Within seconds, the Bedazzlers found themselves standing outside a 24/7 Corner Mart in Jackson Heights. As they glanced around to get their bearings, it was immediately apparent that Doctor Queer had gotten them to the right building. The entire storefront had been smashed in, leaving bricks and glass scattered halfway across the street. Also scattered across the street were the cameras and cameramen who had been providing live footage. One of them was embedded in the side of the Action 5 News van in which he'd arrived. He groaned, partly the result of a spinal injury and partly because his camera lay shattered on the pavement.

Inside the building rumbled a deep growl. Outside, Doctor Queer made neither sound nor motion. He stared straight ahead, frozen in place.

Brooks nudged the doctor. "Are you okay, Arch—"

"Codenames!" Monochrome shouted. "We're in battle. You have to use the codenames!"

"I'm really not okay with the codename," Brooks said.

"Oh?" Monochrome crossed his arms. "Well, I'm suddenly not okay with developing robot bodies."

Brooks sighed. "Are you okay, *Doctor Queer*?"

"He's paralyzed," Monochrome said. "Price of magic and all."

"So the most powerful person on the team is out of commission," Torpedo said.

"Correct," Monochrome said.

"We can't just leave him in the street to get robbed or something," she added.

"No kidding." Monochrome pointed to Human Touch. "HT, you're useless. Stay here and hold onto him."

Agent Brooks, who'd been holding her hand during the teleportation, walked Human Touch over to Doctor Queer. She coughed a little at the patchouli and mildew smell that surrounded the doctor. Hers wasn't the most glamorous of tasks, but it was one that took place in the street, away from the chaos. At further roaring and growling from within the store, she grabbed the doctor's stiff, smelly hand with delight.

Then she had an awful thought, which she articulated. "What if the monster comes out here?"

"It won't. Relax," Monochrome said. He turned to face the building and adjusted his cape. "Okay. Let's do this."

Monochrome led the charge into the store, flanked by Torpedo and Brooks on one side and Blanche and Cactus Jack on the other. As the only one who could fly, Torpedo was also the only one who avoided stepping into a slick menagerie of spilled foodstuffs. Whether it was the grape jelly or the chicken gravy that did it, the rest of the team came tumbling to the ground.

"Man down!" Cactus Jack shouted. Before he landed, he braced for impact using his hands. In an uncomfortable turn of events, the force of the landing drove several of his bone spines back into his body. He curled up, leaned into an empty shelf, and stared at his bloody palms, wincing.

"We haven't even fought anything yet," Monochrome complained, lifting himself off the ground. "You're lucky Blanche is already the group's punching bag."

Blanche perked up at the acknowledgement of her existence.

Brooks, meanwhile, had slid into a pile of tattered flour bags. He stood up, glanced down at his simultaneously sticky and powdery body, and sighed.

Well, I'm enjoying this, Smith said.

Blanche wiped some canned beans from her poncho. "Where'd Torpedo go?"

She received a quick answer when the armored woman blew past her, sailing backward.

"He's strong," Torpedo said as a CLANK signaled her coming to a stop, ass first, in a freezer door. "Really strong."

Torpedo pressed her hands against the doorframe and pushed herself forward. The glass in all six surrounding freezer doors shattered at once, thanks to the vague properties of Zanium.

"Nobody saw that," she said.

Monochrome turned a corner to look for the monster. "Oh, it can't be that bad—"

When it came into view, Torpedo's "really strong" assertion became believable. The purple creature stood nearly nine feet tall. Beneath a bumpy, horned face was the body of an over-steroided bodybuilder: muscles on muscles on muscles in places most people aren't aware muscles exist. In essence, it looked like a Rob Liefeld drawing.* Oddly enough, the only clothed portion of the monster—its pelvic area— was undersized and anatomically incorrect, as if the creature had been censored so an author could avoid describing a monster's dong.

Monochrome, coated in apricot jam, was agitated enough to fight. He jutted his hands out, ready to magmatize the monster. He hoped. His control over his powers was still tenuous, at best.

"Wait," Brooks said.

Monochrome raised an eyebrow. "Why?"

"It's pretty clear we have a Jekyll and Hyde situation,"

---

* If you had to google this, congratulations on getting laid in high school.

Brooks said.

"*How* is that clear?"

"Look at his underwear," Brooks said, pointing.

Monochrome inhaled a laugh. "Of course you were."

Brooks had been a paranormal detective for ten years, and he had been fairly good at it. The lack of confidence irritated him more than the joke. "Would you just..."

As the creature stomped up and down in a tantrum, the Bedazzlers stared at its underpants. They were heather grey boxers, slightly frayed and embroidered MONDAY at the waistband.

Monochrome blinked. "Day of the week underwear? What kind of mediocre—"

"Huh," Torpedo said, getting an idea for an erotic story.

"They're Fruit of the Loom," Blanche said with certainty. "Is that a clue?"

"No, Blanche, that's not a clue," Monochrome said dismissively, then turned to the detective. "Right?"

Brooks shook his head. "No. The tan lines are, though."

Monochrome threw his head back with a laugh. "Of course you were—"

"He wore *glasses*," Brooks snapped.

The monster's craggly face was clearly a lighter purple around the eyes and in a line moving from eye to ear.

"So we probably shouldn't kill him," Monochrome said.

"We shouldn't kill *anyone*," Torpedo said.

Cactus Jack agreed from the floor. "Definitely not."

Out of nowhere, the monster shouted "PIKERS!"

"What the hell does that mean?" Monochrome asked.

The monster continued ranting as it tipped shelves and threw packages of paper plates. "BRAFLAY! MATO!"

"He's not attacking us," Torpedo noted. "He hit me because I tried to blast him with Zanium rays. Ever since, he's just been knocking stuff over like he's looking for—"

The realization hit her and Brooks at the same time.

Brooks directed Blanche. "Get a shopping basket."

"How come?" Blanche asked.

"Just do it," Brooks said.

Blanche scurried off.

"I'm getting pie crust," Torpedo said, jetting off toward frozen foods.

"Bran Flakes," Brooks said, running to the destroyed cereal aisle.

"I have no idea what's going on," Monochrome said.

Blanche reappeared with a basket. "Got it!"

"GREYFROO!" the monster shouted.

Brooks tossed the cereal in Blanche's basket. "Get a grapefruit and a tomato."

Blanche obliged, stepping just outside of the monster's reach to pick the produce off the floor.

"JERCE! TAMPONS!"

"I understood that one," Monochrome said, as it dawned on him what his teammates were doing. "I'll get the juice."

"Already on it," Torpedo said, flying by. "Grab the tampons."

Monochrome winced. "Do I have to?"

"*Oh my God*," Brooks said. "What kind of mediocre—"

"I'll do it," Blanche said, handing Monochrome the basket. "Freaking cripes."

With the basket full, the group convened.

"Who wants to give it to him?" Torpedo asked.

Heh, Smith said.

You probably would, Brooks snipped.

"I'll do it," Monochrome said. "Lead by example and—"

"Why start now?" Brooks asked.

Monochrome approached the monster with the basket extended. "Excuse me. I think this is what you're looking for."

"TAMPONS!"

With an audible SLAP, the creature swatted Monochrome away. The greyscale hero managed to keep the basket upright as he sailed across the produce aisle. He dusted himself off and approached again, this time with a slight limp.

"Yeah, we got the tampons. Bran Flakes too. Grapefruit. Tomato. Pie crust."

The monster raised its fists. "JERCE?"

"Yeah, there's juice."

"Jerce," the monster said, its voice becoming softer.

"Jerce." Monochrome shook his head. "Juice, I mean. Juice."

With that, the creature began to shrink. Muscles folded into muscles, which folded into muscles beneath those. The forehead horns sank back into the monster's skull, his skin cleared, and soon Doug Daniels stood in the wrecked Corner Mart in his underwear, panting and holding a basket of groceries.

He blinked, trying to focus without his glasses. "What happened? Where am I?"

"I know you," Monochrome said. "You're that guy who got the acid bath."

"The what?" Doug asked.

"Yeah, you should be dead," Monochrome said.

Doug glanced from hero to hero. "I'm not dead. What happened?"

"What's the last thing you remember?" Torpedo asked.

"I was heading to the grocery store, and there was an accident with some trucks. Then I woke up here. Why am I in my underwear?" He looked out the shattered storefront. "Is this *Queens*?"

"I don't know if we'll be able to explain it," Brooks said, "but I guess you had some unfinished business. You turned into a monster until we got all the items on your grocery list."

"You're all acting like that's not weird," Doug said.

There was a collective shrug.

"Here," Cactus Jack said, joining them. He handed Doug his hole-riddled jacket to cover more than the embroidered underpants could.

"Thanks," Doug said.

Monochrome limped over to lean a whisper into Cactus Jack's ear. "I'm going to bill you for the replacement."

Doug panicked. "Are you hurt? Did I hurt anyone?"

Monochrome turned back to him and continued pretending he was a leader. "I'm fine, and I'm sure those journalists you chucked will be okay. We'll check in with you every once in a while to make sure it doesn't happen again. Is that okay?"

"Yeah, sure," Doug said, still baffled.

"What's your name again?" Monochrome asked.

"Doug Daniels."

Monochrome's hands began to glow. "Get him out of my sight."

"What?" Torpedo wondered.

Monochrome balled his fists, trying to will the magma away. "Get him out. *Now.*"

"What's the problem?" Blanche asked.

"I hate alliterative names," Monochrome said.

"Are you serious?" Cactus Jack asked.

"I'm very serious," Monochrome said, glowing harder.

"Come on, Doug," Brooks said, escorting the man out of the store.

"Abby?" Monochrome asked.

"Codenames!" she shouted in her best Monochrome impression.

"*Torpedo?* Could you—"

She nodded and jutted her arms forward. "Hot Stuff, fire extinguisher."

A blast from her hands cooled his, and Monochrome dusted himself off.

Outside, two reporters with working cameras had regained consciousness and began circling Doctor Queer and Human Touch.

"Is he okay?" one asked.

Human Touch glanced at Doctor Queer. "He's fine."

"Can you explain what happened?" another asked.

"Not really," Human Touch said. She hadn't seen a thing.

Monochrome emerged from the building with a triumphant jump and a less triumphant landing on his injured left leg. "We defeated the monster! That's what happened. Tell everyone." He knelt down and grabbed at his calf. "Yes, I *was* heroically wounded, and I'd do it again. That's just the price of heroism."

The reporters looked around. "Well... where is it?"

Monochrome stared in confusion that the group wasn't bowing down to worship him. "Where's *what*?"

"The monster..."

"Gone," Monochrome said.

"Just 'gone'?" a reporter asked.

Monochrome watched as Brooks escorted Doug into a cab.

"Yep. Just gone. We banished it."

"Anything else?" a reporter asked.

"Yeah." Monochrome chuckled. "We're going to need a cleanup on Aisle 9."

No one laughed.

6

THE OTHER HALF IS PUBLIC RELATIONS

For someone who formed a superhero team for the sole purpose of improving his PR, Godwin Zane had a terrible understanding of PR. His flippant joke outside the Corner Mart fell flat, and the media soon found a host of other reasons to object to the Bedazzlers. After showering away jams and gravies and changing into normal clothes, they gathered in the Bedazzlestation's Situation Room to watch the news. The last two to enter were Abby and Ana, and Zane was tickled.

"Did you two have to shower together?" he asked.

The women took seats opposite Monochrome and stared him down.

Doctor Queer shook his head. "Godwin, no..."

"Godwin, yes," Zane said. "I didn't even think about that when I roomed you together." He put a hand to his chin. "I should have installed cameras."

Abby's mild pleasure with how he'd handled the Aisle 9 situation vanished.

"Are you done?" she asked.

Zane sat with his injured leg propped up on the table and dressed in a HealWrap™. It looked like a regular cast, but every inch was covered with interlocking Z's and I's in Zane Industries' proprietary serif font. He reached for a remote.

"Yeah, I'm done. Speaking of cameras, let's see how much people love us now."

The first channel he selected was a disappointment. Fifteen minutes of news passed without a single mention of their team. There had, however, been a three-minute segment devoted to Defense Squad Z, who had been presented Presidential Medals of Freedom for their brave effort to hold up a crumbling overpass and clear it of cars before its collapse. On screen, the team's leader, a chubby scientist named Hudson Marrow (a.k.a. the Immortal Man), knelt to receive his medal. The crowd went wild. Six citizens owed their lives to Defense Squad Z.[*]

Zane could no longer stand listening to the media fellate his rivals, and he turned the channel. This one showed more promise.

"—According to a press release, Zane is calling his group the Bedazzlers and their purpose is to use their superpowers to stop threats that powerfree humans cannot. When—"

"Powerfree?" Jack wondered.

Abby answered matter-of-factly. "They're reclaiming it. If you say 'powerless' it seems like they're lacking something."

"They *are* lacking something," Zane noted. "Powers."

They should call them muggles, Smith said.

No, Brooks said.

Tell them, Smith said.

No. When you get a new body, you can make all the bad jokes and references you want.

The newscaster continued. "—many are blaming the so-called Bedazzlers for destroying a local staple that had been in operation since 1925."

The screen cut to the store's owner giving a tearful interview. "They say it's going to cost three million dollars to

---

[*] The overpass was in Iowa.

repair the store. I don't have insurance, so I'm just going to have to close it. Thirty years of my life—gone. Just like that. It's hard to—" He broke down and couldn't continue.

Zane raised a finger. "That's not our fault."

"—We spoke to one man who was traumatized at the scene," the newscaster said.

On screen, Doug Daniels spoke to a reporter. "I woke up in this grocery store in *Queens* and they told me I was a purple monster. I don't know. It doesn't seem right. It seems like someone must have drugged me and put me there, and... they were weird."

"Weird?" the reporter asked.

Zane stood and scoffed at the screen. "*Weird?*"

On screen, Doug nodded. "One guy had spikes, and the black lady had armor, and there was an old guy in a cape who wouldn't move. I kinda feel like they did something to me. The superhero thing is a perfect cover-up story. I mean, Monochrome's been telling people he has powers for years but he never did anything with them."

"I'm really not that old," Doctor Queer complained. "The previous Divine Dimensionmaster lived to be over three hundred."

Abby spoke under her breath. "Damn it, Doug."

Zane clenched his fists. "He can't help it. I told you. People with alliterative names—"

The newscaster droned on. "Furthermore, recently uncovered cell phone footage of an accident earlier this week shows Monochrome blasting a truck with fire—"

"Magma," Zane grumbled.

"—until it exploded and rained chemicals on none other than Mr. Daniels. Some speculate that the billionaire may have it out for this man for one reason or another..."

Everyone stared at Zane.

"Okay. He's a little my fault," he said, "but if I didn't hit the trucks, they were going to hit me. It was an accident."

The newscaster played footage of Doug's accident—taken by a bystander on the scene—then displayed a graph. "We asked our viewers via Facebook and Twitter what they thought of the team, and this is the response we received from over seven thousand votes."

DO YOU APPROVE OF THE BEDAZZLERS?

83% NO
12% YES
4% GO F*CK YOURSELF
1% UNDECIDED

"As you can see," the newscaster said, "if these people are the heroes they claim to be, they have a lot of work to do to convince the American public."

"Well, that's great," Zane said. "When I announced the team, we had twenty-one percent approval. We just stopped a rage monster, and now it's *nine percent lower.*"

"That's how these things go sometimes," Abby said.

"I'm surprised only four percent told the pollsters to go fuck themselves," Brooks said.

"Well, what do we do now?" Zane asked. "Hold a charity fundraiser or—"

"You'd probably do something messed up there too," Jack said. "Let's just wait until this story blows over. There are probably thousands of powered freaks out there. The city's going to keep getting attacked."

Abby agreed. "Let's not dig a hole. We might win favor on the next one."

"Might, schmight. I'm going to call another press conference—"

Doctor Queer raised a hand. "Let's call a vote."

"A what?" Zane asked. "What kind of organization do you think—"

The doctor crossed his arms, tilted his head, and made a face that wordlessly conveyed "fucking listen to me, you ass-hole."

Zane, though an asshole, listened. He spoke deliberately, trying to convince himself of his words. "Yes. We're a team. Everyone's opinion matters. Even Blanche's." He sighed. "We'll hold a vote. All those in favor of giving a press conference?"

He raised his own hand. Nobody else did.

"*Really*? Fine. All those in favor of hanging around waiting for something to happen?"

Everyone but Blanche raised their hands.

"Blanche?" Zane asked.

"Oh, I'm good with whatever you all decide," she said.

Zane rolled his eyes. "Of course you are."

And so the Bedazzlers waited. A lack of news was good for the city and for people in general, so hoping something terrible would happen felt wrong. Still, they hoped for something a little bit terrible. Nothing major that caused loss of life, of course, but mass hypnosis forcing people to pay the costumed ruffians in Times Square or finding out the mayor was in cahoots with shapeshifters would have been just fine.

7

REBRANDED

The mayor of New York City was in cahoots with shapeshifters. And vampires. Zombies, too. He didn't know any of this as he sat in a meeting at the headquarters of the Reticent. The company—ostensibly a medical research firm but actually a paranormal investigation firm—had a long history dating back to the 1790s. Its extensive track record of stopping world-threatening events meant nothing now. What was once a high-tech building teeming with agents like Brooks and Smith had been reduced to a handful of tents at an abandoned construction site.

Thanks to some fine print in the organization's insurance, it could no longer afford to rebuild what was lost when the aptly named Six Block Disaster consumed a six-block radius of Manhattan. And thanks to mysterious interference at City Hall (read: a series of spiteful bribes from a chastened grey billionaire), the permit to rebuild had been revoked anyway. A year of working from tattered tents had driven most employees to leave. The few that persevered through that, having gone unpaid for over a month, had quit. One weird guy kept showing up to work anyway, but he just sat on a bench feeding pigeons.

The mayor spoke as he stood to leave. "I'll see what I can do about the construction permits, but I don't make any promises."

Heidi Werewith, President and CEO of the hollow

organization, escorted him to the door, smiling. "Thank you so much for taking the time to visit us. I do apologize about the tent."

When he was through the doorway, she did her best to slam the door flap shut. It didn't make a sound, and she rolled her eyes, hard. Heidi looked like the sort of woman who would run a Mary Kay business out of her home. There was nothing threatening about her, on the outside. On the inside, however, Agatha Werewith's forty-something niece possessed the same ruthlessness that had made her aunt a success in the role Heidi now held. The late Agatha Werewith successfully ran Reticent operations for two years before she died. The remaining board members (a.k.a. everyone at the company) decided it was Agatha's death that had blown everything to hell and decided to install Heidi in hopes that nepotism would make the company great again.

Seated around a large foldout table covered in coffee stains were the board members:

The Weber triplets (Brandon, Abandon, and Sarandon). To borrow a description from another book, the Webers were unsettling. They were a pale, bald, emaciated group and each one had a different form of heterochromia. When lined up in alphabetical order, their eyes made a smooth transition from blue to green to brown and back to blue. No one was sure whether they were brothers, sisters, a combination, or space aliens. Each bore a striking resemblance to Benedict Cumberbatch.

Travis Marsh. Once Brooks and Smith's boss, Marsh died at Agatha Werewith's hands just before she herself expired. He got better, if becoming a zombie can be considered better. He'd been undead long enough to smell like a compost heap and was kept in the corner of the tent, away from everyone else. He rolled away the oversized dry erase board he'd been using for cover during the mayor's visit, and one of his fingers fell to the ground in the process.

Tarif Baig, a former bail bondsman who gained stretching powers in the same incident that gave most of the Bedazzlers their abilities. His power was widely renounced as "creepy" and "gross," so he'd developed quite the complex about it. He pulled at his fingers one by one like they were Stretch Armstrong dolls, daring someone to say something. Nobody did; they just tried not to look at him.

Mallory Mack. Formerly a nurse, she was forced to quit after the rift incident when her patients' medicine began changing flavors to taste like everything from beef bouillon to beef jerky to beef gravy. That's when she realized she had the ability to alter people's perceptions of flavor. That's also when she realized that her favorite food was beef. Dressed in black, hunched over and frowning, she could have been a background dancer for the Cure, if the Cure were the type of band to have background dancers.

Arlen Samson, Mallory's visual equivalent. That is, he could alter people's perceptions of color. For a construction worker, poor control over this ability presented problems. Namely, lights that appeared green to one person appeared red to another. Cones meant to be an easy-to-spot orange were rendered camouflaged. Several of his coworkers and a few pedestrians were injured before his company realized what was going on and fired him.

Tecumseh Jackson. Discovered in the flooded basement of Reticent headquarters, Jackson was what remained of a terrible experiment. The intent was to bring a strong military mind through a time portal to offer advice. After a long, un-civil debate, it was to be either Stonewall Jackson or William Tecumseh Sherman, but the researchers couldn't decide. They agreed to bring both men into the future, but instead of opening two portals, they yanked half of each from his deathbed. Their bodies fused, and what emerged was half-Union, half-Confederate, and all crazy. He leaned back in his chair, lost in contemplation and tenting his fingers.

Sarah Daniels, wife of the monster known to the media as Aisle 9. The Reticent offered her husband Doug a spot on their board because, frankly, it was empty and no one else wanted to take it. Bylaws were bylaws, and they needed nine members to vote. They also had a vendetta against Brooks and Smith, and figured that Doug deserved a reward for making Brooks's superhero team look like assholes on television. Unfortunately, being a board member was too exceptional for Doug, and he didn't want it. But Sarah was pissed at the Bedazzlers for tormenting her husband, so she signed right up.

There was no pay, but there was a thin promise of it. Each member of the board, full of spite in his or her own way, had been guaranteed a chance to lash out at the world and *maybe* make some money in the process. Nobody else was hiring them, so *maybe* was better than *no*.

"That idiot," Werewith said of the mayor. "He'll never get the permit changed."

"Why did you even brrrrraaaai—brrring it up then?" Marsh asked.

Werewith sneered. "To make it look like we're trying to legitimize this business again."

Her actual plan was to delegitimize the Reticent. Saving the world had never been profitable, and it hadn't gotten the organization anywhere. If they were going to do anything—good or bad—they needed money, and the easiest way to get it was through crime. It was only a matter of figuring out which crime would be the most lucrative.

Tecumseh's suggestion that they steal and resell slaves was met with appalled silence.

The Webers were inclined to rob a children's hospital, but that was deemed too evil.

"We need something we won't get caught doing," Werewith said.

"I guess open robbery is out, then," Mack said.

Werewith took her seat at the head of the table. "Not necessarily."

"What do you mean?" Baig asked.

"You have powers, right?" Werewith asked.

Baig nodded.

The Webers giggled.

"Powers," one said.

"Powers," another whispered.

Werewith turned to Mack. "So do you, right?"

She gave a sullen nod.

The Webers giggled again.

Werewith turned to Samson. "And you?"

He nodded.

The Webers giggled once more.

Werewith ignored their general creepiness. "It seems to me that there are a ton of you freaks running around these days. If we get creative with the robberies, we can use that to our advantage."

"Advantage," all three Webers said with eerie synchronization. Then they giggled.

8

TRAFFIC JAM

While the word cafeteria normally brings to mind rows upon rows of hot buffet food in metal containers basking under light bulbs, the Bedazzlers started their day around a twelve-foot round table eating generic oat puff cereal from plastic Monochrome bowls. A dashing cartoon version of the magma-spewing hero—posing with his fists at his hips and his cape waving—was printed in the bottom of each bowl.

Jack spotted the cartoon as he prepared to fill his bowl with oat puffs. "Dude. Really?"

"I know what you're thinking," Zane said. "You're thinking I'm so arrogant that I picked the bowls with my picture in them on purpose to brag."

Jack was taken aback for a moment. "Yeah, actually."

Zane explained. "My cartoon got canceled and nobody wanted the merch anymore, so they sent it back to me. I'm repurposing it."

"Are you repurposing the cereal too?" Abby frowned. "It's stale."

"Well, *obviously*. It's been down here for fifty years."

Everyone stopped eating and pushed their bowls to the center of the table. All but one of the Bedazzlers had seated themselves across from Zane, and their looks of disdain faced him head on. Ana, who was holding Zane's hand, backed as far away from him as possible.

"That was a joke," Zane said. In a rare moment of self-reflection, he added, "Can you guys really not tell the difference?"

"There were skeletons everywhere when we got here," Jack pointed out.

The group resumed nibbling at their stale breakfast.

"Speaking of food poisoning—" Abby looked at Ana. "When is your assistant going to be over it?"

"Yeah, passing you around is getting old," Zane said.

"She's been hospitalized," Ana said. "Apparently it's pretty serious."

"The food in Zane Tower is that bad?" Jack asked. He always brought his own lunch, so he didn't know.

"Not my fault," Zane said. "I had to cut the food budget to fund this little venture here." He extended a hand as if to show off the dusty cafeteria. "Some countries don't have great food inspection standards, so here were are."

"That's... your fault," Jack said.

"I thought you'd be makin' a killing on The Afterlife™," Blanche said, motioning at Brooks. "Obviously it works."

Make a killing, Smith repeated, chuckling to himself in Brooks's mind.

You never stop, Brooks sighed.

What else do I have to do in here but provide color commentary?

"Oh, it works," Zane said. "It works so well we're currently defending over four hundred lawsuits from families saying we caused them or their deceased loved ones 'undue stress.'"

"That's a simplification," Jack said. "A lot of them are actually claiming unlawful imprisonment."

Zane sighed. "Whatever it is, we had to shut it down. And everyone's boycotting the rest of my products on account of the rift I *didn't* cause and the shitty abilities I *didn't* give people."

"You kinda did give the abilities, though," Blanche said.

Abby spoke directly to Zane. "Your money's not all tied

up in Zane Industries, right?"

"No, of course not. I was rich before I started it, and I'll be rich when it goes under. I'm not looking forward to laying off sixty-four thousand people, though."

The non-Zane Bedazzlers exchanged rapid glances.

"That's... empathetic," Abby said. She pulled out her tablet and took some notes.

"Yeah," Ana agreed. "Weird."

The others nodded.

"Honestly." Zane stood and threw his hands in the air, shirking Ana. "I'm not evil, for crying out loud. You don't have to act surprised that I'm a human being."

"Mr. Zane—" Ana choked. She fanned herself and tried to catch her breath.

He paced and continued ranting. "My employees think I'm an asshole. The public thinks I'm an asshole. I'm sure you all would have loved being the only grey kid in the entire world growing up." He paid no attention to Ana falling backward off her seat. "I'm sure you'd have had a wonderful time at boarding school. I'm sure you'd all be perfectly well-adjusted if your parents kept giraffes in *your* back yard."

Doctor Queer interrupted with a shout of "Godwin!" as he rushed around the table to Ana and took her hand.

"Damn it," Zane said. "I *am* an asshole."

"Well, the first step in recovery is admitting you have a problem," Brooks said.

"I will end you," Zane warned.

Brooks rolled his eyes. "Yeah, sure."

His bluff called, Zane came up with a more believable threat. "Fine. I'll bang your boyfriend again."

"Husband," Brooks corrected.

"Fake marriage," Zane said. In his world, if something didn't receive press coverage, it didn't happen.

"You officiated—"

"Are you okay?" Abby interrupted, speaking far too loud

on purpose.

Zane and Brooks stopped bickering and turned to Ana.

"I'm fine," Ana said, her voice as calm as ever. She wasn't sure exactly how long she could survive without touching someone but it was at least eighty seconds, her personal record.

"This is an alert. This is a bedazzalert. Get your lazy asses to the Situation Room."

"Okay, hold up," Jack said. "Who sounds the alert if you're here right now?"

"It's an automated system that scans the radio and news," Zane said. "You didn't think I was sitting around waiting to tell you guys about a crime, did you?"

They did, in fact, think that.

"I have a job, even if it is to go down with my ship."

They all rose from their chairs, ready for action.

"Breakfast, though..." As Jack trailed off, he gave his half-full cereal bowl a wistful gaze.

With most of the team already out the door, Blanche rallied a useless "let's go!"

In the Situation Room, the Bedazzlers faced six new headlines:

LIVE: MIDTOWN TRAFFIC JAM
WRECKS IN THE CITY
BREAKING: HEAVY CONGESTION, ACCIDENTS
TRÁFICO MALÉFICO
COMMUTERS IN A JAM
SOCIALISM CAUSES TRAFFIC JAM

"This doesn't really seem like it's in our wheelhouse,"

Brooks said.

"Well, the automated alerts can't all be winners," Zane said.

"Wait," Jack said. "What's with *that* guy?"

The newscasters didn't seem to notice, but on one street corner stood a man outfitted in black spandex from neck to toe. On his chest were three large dots: red at the top, yellow in the middle, and green at the bottom. He wore a domino mask and had all the appearance of a lame villain who is defeated early in a story as a test of the heroes' mettle and a distraction from the bigger plot.

"There's a huge traffic jam, and this guy just happens to be dressed like a traffic signal?" Abby asked. "I don't think so."

Zane took charge. "Costumes on, people. Arch, get ready to teleport us again."

Doctor Queer sighed.

Several minutes and one "*Movens non moveatur*" later, the Bedazzlers arrived at the northwest corner of 56th and 5th to a chorus of HONNNNNNNKs. Human Touch, prepared to do her part, was already holding Doctor Queer's hand when they got there. Having missed the chance to finish breakfast and landing only a few feet from a kebab cart, hunger hit her hard and fast, and she waved her free hand until she caught the proprietor's attention.

"Ugh," Brooks said, eyeing Trump Tower.

Cactus Jack laughed. "You gotta admit it's funny watching him waste everyone's time."

"I actually hope he wins the primaries and turns the Republican Party into a complete joke," Brooks said. "Can you imagine how easily Hillary would beat him?"

"Three hundred electoral votes, easy," Torpedo said.

The three New Yorkers shared a deep, hearty laugh—unable to contemplate any other possibility.

Unlike in most cases, the situation on the ground was worse than it seemed on TV. Not a single car moved in any direction, and there were twelve rage-induced fender benders at this intersection alone. Some drivers had been stuck so long that they'd abandoned their vehicles. Others were asleep at the wheel. An ambulance, sirens blaring, scuffled down the sidewalk, its driver sticking his head out the window to politely request that pedestrians "get the fuck out of the way." As Human Touch awkwardly maneuvered a one-handed exchange of money for kebab, the ambulance plowed through the cart, sending her snack to the ground. The kebab salesman, gesturing and shouting, went chasing after the ambulance.

"Hey!" Monochrome shouted, spotting the spandex-wearer across the street. "There he is!"

Even though traffic wasn't moving, everyone honked at the group as they crossed 56th. The honks served only to relieve a tiny bit of tension in the honkers.

"What are you doing?" Monochrome asked, looking up.

At 5'10", Monochrome was average height, but he was positively twee next to this man. So were Cactus Jack and Agent Brooks, the taller members of the team. The traffic light-inspired villain stood around 6'8" and, despite the minimizing effect spandex has on muscles, was completely ripped. What little skin was exposed appeared to be sunburned and peeling, which made sense paired with the man's vibrant red hair.

The costumed villain scoffed. "I'm just minding my own business. Like you should be."

"Okay, but you're obviously doing something with the lights," Monochrome said.

"Am I?" the man asked.

"Yes. Yes you are. Look." Monochrome glanced up at the

nearest traffic light and pointed. Every light in the intersection was red, including the pedestrian walk signals. Outside Trump Tower, a crowd of frustrated tourists was backed up for blocks. A few peed into a trashcan.

"Am I?" the man repeated.

"Oh my God. What are you, twelve?" Monochrome asked.

"Stop doing what you're doing," Torpedo said. She tried to appeal to the man's reason. "Ambulances can't get by. You're hurting people."

"Am I?" the man repeated.

Monochrome tried to provoke him. "Yes, you unfathomable douche!"

There was a short silence. "*Am* I?"

"Can I punch him?" Monochrome turned to the group's attorney.

Cactus Jack sighed. "No. According to New York law, citizens can only use force in a citizen's arrest if there is certainty that an offender has actually committed a crime."

"Pissing with traffic lights is a crime, right?"

Cactus Jack nodded. "Tampering with public property and obstructing government administration."

"Perfect," Monochrome said. He stared up at the man, attempting to intimidate. "Confess."

"Why would I do that?" the man asked. "He just said you can't do anything unless you have proof I committed a crime."

"Ugh," Monochrome said. "What's your name?"

The villain smirked. "They call me Traffic Jam."

Monochrome shook his hands, trying to calm himself out of producing magma. "For the love of—"

"So you call yourself Traffic Jam," Brooks said. "And we're looking at the biggest traffic jam New York has ever seen—"

Torpedo finished his thought. "—And you're saying you have nothing to do with it?"

"*Am* I?" Traffic Jam asked.

The back-and-forth between the Bedazzlers and Traffic Jam continued for some time.

While cars and pedestrians alike were hindered by the record-breaking traffic jam, the First National Bank of Money went woefully understaffed. Low wages meant that most of the bank's tellers lived deep in New Jersey and commuted to work, and they couldn't make it in on time that day. With just one person manning the counter, it was a breeze for a pair of robbers to slip in and demand that she turn over stacks upon stacks of money. The teller managed to hit the panic button, but the NYPD was also held up in traffic.

Brooks, Torpedo, and Cactus Jack had given up and seated themselves on a curb as Monochrome continued to antagonize and be antagonized by Traffic Jam. They'd been waiting so long that Doctor Queer emerged from his paralysis and joined them, Human Touch in hand.

"What's going on?" Human Touch asked.

Torpedo sighed. "They just keep arguing."

"I'm hungry," Cactus Jack complained.

"I'm bored," Brooks complained.

I'm noncorporeal, Smith complained.

Doctor Queer took the conversation in a solemn direction. "I'm worried that my legacy will be one of failure, and that after three hundred years this world will collapse into darkness and peril."

"That's a bummer," Blanche said.

"Yeah. Damn," Cactus Jack said.

"Wait a minute," Torpedo said, Doctor Queer's confession giving her an idea. "Remember when Zane was acting weirdly sympathetic earlier?"

The group nodded.

Behind them, Monochrome didn't hear Torpedo's failure to use his codename. He was too busy shouting at Traffic Jam, still trying to provoke a reaction. "*Unfathomable* douche! Your costume is the stupidest thing I've ever seen!" He didn't realize that petty insults—the kind that triggered his magma—did nothing to others.

Brooks perked up and turned to Torpedo. "I think I get you."

"I don't," Blanche said.

Torpedo turned to Human Touch. "See if you can hold Traffic Jam's hand."

Doctor Queer escorted HT to where the villain and Monochrome continued their argument. He'd been friends with Godwin Zane long enough to establish a code. A certain head tilt meant "shut the fuck up and roll with this."

He tilted his head as he butted between Monochrome and Traffic Jam. Monochrome shut up and rolled with it.

"Excuse me," the doctor said. "I need to use the restroom. Can you hold her hand for a moment?"

Traffic Jam blinked. "What?"

"Her superpower is trash," Monochrome said. "She has to touch someone at all times or she dies."

"That sucks." He glanced at the curb. "But you have a whole team."

Monochrome pointed at his bored teammates one by one, rattling off excuses for why the others couldn't hold her hand. "Armor, cyborg, bone spines, can't expose her skin or we'll all go blind..."

"What about you?" Traffic Jam asked.

Monochrome glanced down at his hands, already emitting

a soft glow. "I'm bound to melt something any minute now."

Traffic Jam sighed and took Human Touch's hand. "Fine."

Monochrome continued berating him. "Anyway, if you would just admit you're doing this, we could all go home."

"I'm home at three o'clock either way," Traffic Jam said.

"What's at three o'clock?" Monochrome asked.

"*Doctor Phil*," Traffic Jam said.

"You've got to be kidding."

"What? The guy has a lot of good advice."

"The guy's a sham. HT?"

Human Touch shrugged to show her lack of opinion on the matter. She hadn't watched broadcast television since she was a child and found the whole concept vexing.

"For your information," Traffic Jam said, "today's episode is about dealing with superpowers. You know, like the ones you gave a bunch of people without asking them."

"I didn't do it," Monochrome said. "It was a setup. The FBI held six separate investigations. I spoke before Congress. Nobody can find any evidence of wrongdoing. You know why?"

"Because you're—"

"Because there was no wrongdoing!" Monochrome's hands were at a full glow now. "Torpedo?"

The armored Bedazzler couldn't hear him over all the honking.

"*Torpedoooo!*" he screamed.

She approached and obliged him with a quick, extinguishing spray.

"See?" Traffic Jam said. "You could benefit from today's *Phil* too."

"Nobody benefits from *Doctor Phil*."

Traffic Jam looked genuinely hurt. "You know what your problem is?"

"You?" Monochrome wondered.

Torpedo was about to leave, but instead motioned for the

others to join her. Watching Monochrome get chewed out wouldn't solve their hunger, but it might at least solve their boredom.

The villain shook his head. "You're so rich it doesn't matter you have shitty powers. You don't know what it's like for your kid to tell all her friends grass is orange because you screwed with her eyes. You don't know what it's like to lose your job because you made a stop sign blue and people crashed because they didn't notice it. It helps that you don't care about anyone but yourself..."

The Bedazzlers who weren't Monochrome nodded along.

Traffic Jam sobbed. "How am I supposed to pay child support when I can't hold a job?"

Monochrome was unmoved. "I feel like there are definitely jobs your power doesn't affect..."

As Traffic Jam continued confessing his troubles, the traffic lights began blinking all three colors at once. There was a loud, collective HONNNNNNNNNNNNNK as drivers attempted to interpret that.

"If you were me, maybe you'd be working petty crimes too," Traffic Jam sniffed.

"Petty crimes like what?" Monochrome asked.

"Like this." Traffic Jam gestured at the nearest light. "Red." It turned red. "Yellow." It turned yellow. "Green." It turned green.

Monochrome turned to Torpedo. "Has Hot Stuff been recording this?"

"She records everything. And now that I think about it, that's really troubling."

"Great." Monochrome wound up his now-cool fist and punched Traffic Jam in the face.

Cactus Jack threw up his hands. "Dude. He was calming down."

"Yeah, well... I hate him."

Traffic Jam recovered. "I'm gonna make you wish you

never—"

He flung Human Touch from his arm. Doctor Queer scooped her up and gestured at the villain with his free hand. A teal glow emerged. "*Somnum dulce.*"

Traffic Jam collapsed against a brick wall, fast asleep, and all the traffic lights in New York returned to their normal functionality. Traffic went back to being unbearable rather than impossible, and Doctor Queer swayed back and forth, trapped in a state of hypnagogia.

Monochrome snapped his fingers in front of the doctor's face, to no avail. Their primary method of transportation out of commission, the Bedazzlers were faced with few options. Cactus Jack took Human Touch's hand, Brooks threw Traffic Jam over his shoulder, Torpedo carried Doctor Queer, and the group began the long trek back to Zane Tower.

Just outside the First National Bank of Money, two hired guns loaded their last few stacks of bills into a bicycle basket.

One robber turned to the other. "Easy."

Suddenly, a car blew by them.

"Um, I thought the jam was supposed to last another hour," the other said.

Panic hit the first robber's eyes. "It was. We gotta move."

A finger tapped his shoulder. "Where you going with that?"

"I—" He turned to find three officers, freshly unimpeded.

"You're under arrest," one said.

9

OBJECTION!

The walk back had been interrupted by no fewer than six news crews—not to mention the detour to turn Traffic Jam in to police—and had taken the team over three hours. By the time they shuttled back over to the Bedazzlestation, Doctor Queer had come to.

"Did it work?" he asked.

"It could have been less annoying," Brooks said.

"The good news," Abby said, "is that there was no property damage."

"And that Ana has a power," Blanche said, offering her hand up for a high five.

Ana declined.

The Bedazzlers weren't entirely sure what her power was yet, but suffice it to say it had something to do with getting people to spill their inner turmoil. The group cheered in agreement. Ana blushed and lowered her head to avoid the attention.

Monochrome offered disinterest. "Yeah, sure. Whatever. The important thing is they can't blame us for anything on this one."

He was wrong.

Their hunger satiated by off-brand potato chips, the group once again sat in the Situation Room, taking in the monitors. A credit to both capitalism and collusion, every station aired commercials at the same time. The audio playing in the room was from one featuring an obvious con man with slicked-back hair and a suit decked with comic-style POW! bubbles who stood at the edge of the Hudson River.

"Have *you* been injured in a bizarre incident?" he asked. "Did a superpowered freak destroy *your* home? Did *you* wake up one morning to find yourself invisible? Invincible? Irascible?" He pointed directly at the camera. "You're not to blame!" His location changed to an accident site on the New Jersey Turnpike. As smoke billowed from a tractor-trailer, he continued. "The world is changing." In the background, a man in a gorilla costume fought a man in a lizard costume. The effects weren't quite as convincing as 1960s television. "*You* shouldn't have to change with it. Call 800-IWASWRONGED for a free consultation. And remember: at Bergman and Fox, if it doesn't go your way, you don't pay!"

"I thought superheroism would involve a lot more punching and a lot less sitting around watching the news," Brooks said. "Not that I'm complaining."

You're complaining, Smith said.

"Resolving things without violence is better," Jack said.

Ana and Doctor Queer nodded.

"Of course it is," Brooks said. "I'm just saying it's a bit anticlimactic. Do we really need a team for thi—"

On screen, the news resumed. A serious, suited newscaster extended a lede. "The biggest question on the streets seems to be: 'Do we really need a team for this?' People are angry. Irene Smolder is on the scene."

At that, Monochrome tapped a button on his phone. The other stations disappeared and Irene's program expanded to fill the entire wall. On the scene—a Manhattan street closed for construction—a large group of beard-laden tie-dye wearers had amassed. Citizens Against Cars (CAC) had been an organization since 1928, and climate change had emboldened them. Their spokesman, who wore a red bandana over his mouth and called himself Jorge de la Coche, bellyached about the Bedazzlers' role in destroying the planet.

"We finally had a traffic jam so enormous that it was set to make people rethink automobile use, and the Bedazzlers ruined it."

"There were genuine concerns with the traffic," Irene said. "For instance, police and ambulances being unable to make it to emergency—"

"The biggest emergency is global warming," Jorge said. "Sometimes you have to break a few eggs." Behind their speaker, several CAC members cheered him on, shaking noisemakers and shouting. Then without warning, they rushed off screen, apparently chasing after a man who'd thrown a plastic bottle into a garbage bin.

Irene moved across the street to speak with another group of concerned citizens.

"I'm worried about vigilantism," an older woman said. "Just because the police can't stop people with superpowers doesn't mean any old Tom, Dick, or Harry has the right to. They should have waited for the government to call Defense Squad Z."

"The Bedazzlers haven't done anything outside the bounds of the law yet," Irene noted.

"Yet," the woman said. "Give it time. I've seen those superhero movies."

Irene accepted that this made the woman an expert and moved on to speak to another angry group: fashion designers. She caught the group of bizarrely dressed men and women on their way into Manhattan's hottest restaurant—2045—and her questions added to their hunger-induced distress.

"Their costumes are garbage," said a woman with eyebrows made of rhinestones.

"Hot garbage," agreed a man with an identically composed moustache.

Zane shook his fists. "Tasteless idiots." He turned to Ana. "This is probably your fault for adding that stupid mask—"

A thin man wearing nothing but an elongated burlap vest spoke next. "The armored lady looks good, though."

The other designers nodded in agreement.

Abby glanced around the room, unable to hide her smirk.

Irene moved on to a pair of tourists in camo hats.

"What do you think about the Bedazzlers?" she asked.

There was a mumble, followed by "bunch of damn New York liberal elites."

"They're complaining about New Yorkers in New York?" Jack wondered. "How New York of them..."

On screen, the man's companion nodded. "Pushing a woke, liberal agenda. There's only one white person on the team and of course he's a homo—"

Brooks scratched his head and spoke to Doctor Queer. "I think he means you."

"Now why would anyone make that assumption?" Doctor Queer asked.

"The name," Jack suggested.

"Maybe the rainbow ascot," Abby noted.

"I'm white," Blanche whined.

No one responded to her complaint.

Finally, Irene spoke to a group of middle-aged women on their way home from Moms at the Movies. Each of the three women angled a stroller, attempting to get their child in the foreground of the shot. Their scowls at each other morphed into exaggerated smiles for the camera.

"I'm not worried about them being vigilantes," mom number one said. "I just don't see how they're very effective."

Mom number two nodded. "How many robberies and murders happened while they were worried about stopping a traffic jam? I saw the police stop a bank robbery while they were putzing around."

Mom number three concurred. "Right. Who is setting their

priorities?"

"Someone with backward priorities, that's who," mom number two said.

The moms went back and forth for a moment, restating the same idea in slightly different ways. Finally, mom number one brought up a salient point. "The thing with Defense Squad Z is, they report directly to the president, so—"

Zane, having heard enough, switched the screens off. "That... could have gone better."

"Any idea what the approval rating is now?" Jack asked.

Abby checked her phone. "Eight percent. And 'go fuck yourself' dropped to three percent." She added, "I think you may have to face the fact that nobody wants the Bedazzlers."

Godwin Zane, who had once invested over a billion dollars into the failed NosePhone™, refused to admit that he could have a bad idea.

"We just need a lucky break," he said.

10

A TASTE OF DISASTER

Godwin Zane did almost everything with flair, from giving a press conference to using a calculator.* When it came to thrills, his personality made him the billionaire who cried wolf. Those who knew him got used to his eccentricity, and they stopped getting excited when it seemed like he had something exciting to say. Still, Brooks was a little bit excited. He'd been called to Zane's Bedazzlestation bedroom for an important conversation, and there was no doubt in his mind that it had something to do with the robot body.

This has to be it, Brooks said. *It's just one step up from the armored suit.*

Smith tried to temper his expectations. *Remember who you're dealing with.*

When he entered the room, Brooks remembered who he was dealing with. Zane had converted the bedroom into an office, which could have been a respectable decision, but his desk was in the center of an eight-by-eight, three-foot deep ball pit. He lay in it with only his head exposed—a striking bit of grey against a field of rainbow-colored plastic balls.

"Okay, so..." Zane started.

Brooks instinctively ignored the conversation's context. "Did you figure out the robot body?"

---

* He put the *sin* in Sin^{-1}

"What?" Zane asked. He raised a hand from the pit to dismiss the notion. "No. Now, I know what you're thinking."

"That—"

Zane didn't let Brooks express what he was thinking. "You're wondering why the balls aren't monochromatic."

"I'm really not," Brooks said.

"Well. I ordered some custom balls from Oriental Trading Company, but—"

Brooks tuned him out. In his mind, he snapped. He and Smith were in The Afterlife™ Simple Farm Life scenario. Brooks hated Simple Farm Life, and Smith, who originally hailed from Indiana, hated it even more. But with only seventy-two scenarios to choose from, there wasn't enough variety to keep any out of rotation. Brooks had been sitting patiently on a tree stump, watching Smith milk a cow. His patience worn, he stood and began flailing.

It's still not done! Brooks kicked a convenient metal pail, and it, in turn, kicked up a plume of dust.

Smith coughed a little and abandoned the cow, which protested with a virtual MOOO.

I told you it wouldn't be done.

I know you did!

So you're mad at me for being right?

Brooks seethed. *I want you out of my head.*

Smith was similarly testy, albeit from the farming. *I know. I've heard. And you know what?*

"—talk to you about something important," Zane said. He noted the cyborg's glazed eyes and tossed a yellow ball at him. "Are you even listening?"

"No," Brooks said. "Shut up."

"Excuse me?" Zane asked.

If you want me out of here, Zane can put me in a computer or the cloud or whatever, Smith said.

You know I trust him about as much as I trust the Coen brothers to make a good movie.

Smith counted facts. *One: Your taste is terrible. Two: Then you need to accept that you are <u>choosing</u> to keep me in here. It's not the worst thing that's ever happened to either of us, and you could stop acting like it is. Treat it like it's permanent and you can only be pleasantly surprised.*

Brooks stood, stunned. *When have you <u>ever</u> been optimistic?*

Never, Smith said. *That's why you need to be.*

"Pay attention to me!" Zane shouted.

Brooks sighed and stared down at the ball pit. "What?"

"What do you think of Abby?" Zane asked.

"Uh, she's fine?" Brooks said.

Zane grinned. "Yeah she is."

"Oh, great," Brooks said, taking a seat in the corner.

Zane stood up to the PLINK PLUNK of plastic balls tumbling back into the pit.

"I'm interested in her," Zane said. He paused for emphasis. "Sexually."

Brooks frowned. "I got that. So you're asking the one gay man on the team for advice?"

Zane stepped out of the pit. "No, I'm asking the only person in a functional relationship for advice."

"It's not really all that functional," Brooks said.

Hey! Smith complained.

Zane pondered out loud. "Do you think she'd ever—"

"No."

"You didn't let me finish."

"No."

"Seriously. What if—"

"No."

"I could—"

"No."

Normally, Zane would have been frustrated to the point of melting something. But the Q.U.E.E.R. Method had done wonders, and he instead resolved his aggravation with an insult. "Your husband thought I was good enough to bang."

Ugh, Brooks and Smith said simultaneously.

"Are you going to keep bringing that up forever?" Brooks asked.

"Maybe," Zane said. "Maybe not if I ever get to sleep with someone else. You can help with that. Tell Abby how awesome I am."

Before Brooks could unleash a lengthy string of insults in return, there was an interruption.

"This is an alert. This is a bedazzalert. Get your lazy asses to the Situation Room."

"Sigh," Zane said, heading for the door.

Brooks followed.

"We'll pick this up later," Zane said.

"No. No we won't."

It was odd for Brooks and Monochrome to enter the room together, and Jack noticed. But before he could make a joke no one would laugh at, the station's televisions went to full blast and newscasters shouted over each other as dramatic headlines filled the screens.

LIVE: WINE TASTING GONE WRONG
PUT A CORK IN IT?
BREAKING: TAINTED WINE
VINO HORRIBLE, OBSTINO INSUFRIBLE
THE GRAPE DEPRESSION: BAD WINE STRIKES
LIVE: WINE TASTING HAVOK, LIBERALS TO BLAME?

Zane tapped a few buttons on his Zanephone to limit the room to one audio source.

A newscaster laid out the situation in a smooth baritone. "Vignault's 2015 is turning out to be a real disaster..."

"What are they talking about?" Ana asked.

"It's a swanky wine tasting party," Zane explained. "Lasts for twenty-four hours. They have one every fall. I'm usually invited, but—"

"But everyone hates you now," Brooks said.

"I'm not much for wine," Blanche offered. "Gimme a can of Schlitz any time."

No one cared about Blanche's preference for beer.

The newscaster of choice went on to explain that all six of the wines sampled so far had been tainted, an unprecedented disaster. Important, rich people were furious about the foul-tasting wine, and this was richly important.

"I don't get it," Jack said.

"Me neither," Abby added.

"What's not to get?" Zane asked.

"Why do we care if some rich people drink crappy wine?" Jack asked.

Zane threw up his hands. "PR! The wealthy mean a lot more than whatever schlubs we can save on the streets. Imagine helping Rupert Murdoch or Michael Bloomberg."

Brooks grimaced. "Do we have to?"

"PR!" Zane shouted again, as if the two letters alone made a compelling argument.

Doctor Queer faced the team members who weren't Zane. "I too doubt the usefulness of this mission, but we aren't incredibly busy at the moment..."

"That's fair," Blanche said. In one day, she had knitted thirteen cat sweaters.

Zane rose from his seat and threw a fist in the air. "To Vignault's!"

"Like this?" Jack asked, tugging at his hole-riddled sweater. "Or in costume?"

Zane reseated himself. "Good point. Go home, make yourselves presentable, and meet me there." He jumped and threw his fist in the air again. "To Vignault's!"

"Where is it?" Abby asked.

Zane deflated into his seat once more. "76th and Madison. The Kirkland Millington Hotel. "

There was a brief silence.

Zane took an apprehensive look around the room. "Any other questions?"

There were none.

"To Vignault's!" he shouted, pumping his fist again.

All of the Bedazzlers knew how to dress for a swanky party except for Blanche. While Zane, Abby, Ana, Brooks, Doctor Queer, and Jack waited in tuxedos and gowns, the team's last member arrived wearing a bisque pantsuit over her usual balaclava, goggles, and gloves combo. She'd made one alteration to the mask, poking a small hole in the top to let some long blonde hair flow.

"Really, Blanche?" Zane asked.

Thinking he was offended by her tardiness, she apologized. "Sorry. It takes a freakin' long time to catch the Staten Island Ferry."

"You can't come in dressed like that," he said.

She hunched in defeat. "Really? I think the hair adds a nice feminine touch."

"Really. Wait here in case we need you to blind someone."

"All right." She seated herself on a bench and pulled out her phone, ready to play a few rounds of Hokeyblock Blast.

"I feel vulnerable and wrong," Doctor Queer said. He hadn't changed out of his divine dimensionmastering costume in decades, and the dusty tuxedo was too snug thanks to some mid-1970s weight gain.

"You smell a lot better, though," Abby said.

Zane eyed her up and down, homing in on her waist.

"Speaking of smells."

Abby crossed her arms. "What?"

"You could have had your dress laundered before you came here."

"What are you talking about?" Abby asked.

"That stain," Zane said, finger pointed.

She pulled at the side of her red dress and squinted. "I don't see anything."

"Ugh. It's super obvious," Zane said.

"Not really," Jack said.

Ana shrugged. "I don't see anything."

"Are you people screwing with me?" Zane asked. "It's huge."

"I don't see it either," Brooks said.

Blanche, always the last to agree, looked up from her phone and agreed. "Nope. No stain."

Zane brought his fists up to his face and tapped his forehead a few times. "It's... fine. Whatever."

"Are we going inside or what?" Jack asked.

"Yes." Zane bent his arm and extended it toward Abby. "Ms..." He forgot her last name.

She took a step back. "What are you doing?"

"People go to Vignault's with dates," Zane said.

Abby broke into a hard laugh. "Yeah, okay." She grabbed the nearest person who wasn't Zane and strolled toward the door, arm-in-arm with Doctor Queer.

Brooks snickered. "Told you." Then he realized Ana and Jack had walked into the lobby together. "Shit."

"Well," Zane said. "I guess I'm gay today."

At least I never went on a date with him, Smith said. *You should have brought flowers.*

I swear I will reformat you.

Brooks and Zane followed the others and walked in together. It didn't take long for their plan—if they ever had one—to go awry. A burly bouncer with a list guarded the entrance to the conference room. None of the Bedazzlers were on the guest list, but one was on the *other* list.

"You're not allowed within fifty yards of this party," the bouncer said to Zane.

"What?"

"It says Godwin Zane is barred for life." He held up the sheet for the group to see.

BANNED:
Andy Dick
Godwin Zane

"I'm not Godwin Zane. I'm... Trevor... Neatly?" He'd always wanted to come up with a false name on the fly, but it didn't come out nearly as cool as he'd imagined.

"Nice try, greyboy."

Zane squinted. "What did you call me?"

"Grey. Boy. Now beat it."

Despite being well aware of his own greyness, Zane didn't appreciate it being pointed out and mocked. As his anger built, his magma bubbled.

"Ow!" Brooks withdrew his arm with a shout. He looked down at his arm and let out a louder shout. "*Oh my God!*"

"You okay?" Abby asked. When she got closer, she let out a "blurrrgggaggggh."

Brooks was not okay. On his left forearm, a three-by-three-inch patch of tuxedo and skin had been burned away, revealing a metallic cyborg interior. It was both a painful injury and an unwanted reminder that he was not human.

Are you going to have an existential crisis again? Smith asked.
I might.
Please don't.
Oh, well... if you put it that way!
"Oops," Zane said.
"Oops?" Brooks repeated. "*OOPS!?*"

"Let's move past it," Zane said.

"Godwin—" Doctor Queer started.

"I'm sorry?" Zane said.

"Not accepted," Brooks said. "You *burned a hole in my arm.*"

A confused Zane tried the opposite statement. "I'm not sorry?"

Hit him, Smith suggested.

Zane shook his head in annoyance. "It's not like we can't just slap a HealWrap™ on it."

"Oh. Well, if you put it that way, I totally don't mind the *hole in my arm.*"

Hit him, Smith suggested again.

Doctor Queer tired of the bickering. He waved a glittering hand at the bouncer to change his mind.

"*Quod dico.* Let us in."

"Looks like you're on the list," the bouncer said, gesturing for them to enter.

"Wait," Abby said. "You don't look like you're in pain."

"Not all magic has a *physical* consequence," Doctor Queer said.

"Well, what's the consequence of that one?" Ana asked.

"I'd rather not say—"

Zane flippantly disregarded the doctor's discomfort. "If he mind controls people, he has to do whatever other people tell him to."

"You're mind controlled too?" Abby asked, a little too excited.

"Keep it down," Doctor Queer said. "Yes. Indeed."

"Get this stain off my dress," Abby said, pointing at her side.

Zane pointed at her. "You did see it!"

"*Mundabit*," Doctor Queer said. The stain disappeared and reappeared on his own shirt.

"Thanks," Abby said.

"We're not here for parlor tricks," Zane groused.

Brooks didn't hesitate to give Doctor Queer an order of his own. "Punch Zane."

The doctor obliged, delivering a fist to Zane's nose.

"Ow!" Zane said, pinching it to hold back the blood. "You son of a—"

"Huh. His blood's red," Jack said. "I always wondered about that."

"Punch him," Zane said, pointing at Brooks.

Doctor Queer did, but it had little effect. The cyborg stared at him, stone-faced.

"Make me normal," Ana blurted.

"I don't know a spell for that," Doctor Queer said.

She sulked. Then an idea hit her. "Research a spell for that?"

"At once!" He turned, left the room, and went home.

Zane spoke with a nasal, pinched-nose voice. "Good job. Now our most powerful member is gone." He eyed Abby with a smirk. "Your date's gone, too."

"Pass," she said, taking Brooks's non-singed arm.

A room of two hundred wealthy and agitated Vignault's patrons stared at the idiots causing a scene in the doorway.

Abby spoke. "We're here to—"

A commotion put a stop to her words. There they were: Defense Squad Z. The Immortal Man, Laser Scream, Horse Whisperer, Steel Foot, The Law, Great Aim, and Admiral Milky Way. Fully costumed, they emerged from the wine cellar with an evildoer in hand. A few of the teammates high-fived each other as they shared a laugh. The room burst into applause as patrons pulled out their phones and rushed to get closer looks.

"Don't worry," The Law said, presenting an embarrassed Goth woman. "This lady right here was making you all think the wine tasted bad so her friends could buy it cheap and make some money."

"Yeah," Great Aim said. "But she fought The Law and

The Law won."

The room exploded in laughter.

"I hate everything," Zane said as a crowd gathered around Defense Squad Z for photos. His "cleanup on Aisle 9" quip was, he believed, better than anything a Z-man had ever said. As with superheroing, they got all the credit when it came to jokes. He kicked at the floor. "Let's get out of here."

Outside, Blanche popped up off the bench. "How'd it go?"

"Could have been better," Jack said.

"Well, that's okay. We'll get our lucky break."

11

A LUCKY BREAK

Ask a person at random whether Coney Island is worth visiting, and the vast majority will ignore you. Those who answer are likely to say "no." That's because most people visit in the summer. In the summer, crowds, heat, humidity, and an abundance of discarded needles make the area's amusement parks unpleasant to visit for anyone who isn't angling to win a hotdog eating contest. In October, the heat and humidity leave and the drug needles are mostly washed away, so it's not so bad. Plus, there's a Halloween theme and abundant pumpkin spice.

It was the ideal place for a team-building exercise. Having witnessed the well-oiled superheroing machine that was Defense Squad Z, the Bedazzlers felt rightly inadequate. After a semi-decent night's sleep and a few hours' practice killing Tom Hankses, they set out to get to know each other better.

For the moment, that meant waiting in line for calorie-heavy carnival food.

"You're paying?" Torpedo asked.

"Of course I'm not paying," Monochrome said. "You think this is a charit—"

Doctor Queer shook his head.

"I'd love to," Monochrome corrected.

A stout, angry man in a tracksuit interrupted the moment. "Nice costumes, assholes."

Monochrome feigned a smile to kill him with kindness

rather than magma. "Thanks. We think so. If you want, I can get you the Aesthetics Department's number—"

The angry man grumbled something and turned back to his friends. Monochrome turned back to the people he wrongly considered his.

"What's everyone getting?" he asked.

Blanche didn't hesitate to answer. "Corn dog."

Everyone stared at her.

"Gross," Human Touch said.

Brooks wasn't as put off. "I don't mind a good—"

Babe, Smith warned.

Brooks stopped himself from finishing his sentence, and Monochrome sank when he realized the cyborg wasn't going to set himself up for a punchline.

"Fries," Torpedo said.

Cactus Jack nodded. "The fries are good."

"Just fries?" Monochrome asked.

"You see anything else vegetarian on the menu?" Torpedo asked.

"You don't eat meat? Hmm. Good to know." Monochrome made a mental note to impress her by being kind to animals later.

When they got up to the window, a pimpled teenager in a striped red and white shirt pointed to some cardboard signage that read "NO CAPES."

"Excuse me?" Monochrome asked.

"We don't serve capes," the kid said. "Store policy."

"You don't have an interior," Monochrome said.

That was true. Snackey's was a walk-up stand, and a dilapidated one at that. It was curious to the Bedazzlers that the stand had any kind of policy.

"Store policy," the kid repeated.

"Just take your cape off," Torpedo said.

"Cape is slang for superhero," the kid said.

"Since when?" Torpedo asked. "I don't wear a cape."

"Neither do I," Human Touch said.

"Nope," Blanche said.

Brooks and Cactus Jack shook their heads.

The kid shrugged. "Store poli—"

"Yes. Store policy. We know," Monochrome said. "I'm sure you can just give us some corn dogs and fries and send us on our way."

"Store polic—"

Behind them, a few people grumbled. One shouted, "Move it along!"

"Sigh," Monochrome said. "Let's go."

The sullen group moved on without snacks.

Monochrome looked over his shoulder at Snackey's. "Your fries are terrible anyway!"

"The fries are great," Cactus Jack sighed.

"Maybe the Dippin' Dots cart will serve us," Human Touch said.

"I freakin' love Dippin' Dots," Blanche said.

Monochrome rolled his eyes. "No one cares, Blanche."

They walked along, and he stopped dead in his tracks. An artist parked on the sidewalk proudly displayed several paintings of Defense Squad Z. They weren't stylistically interesting, but they were abundant. The caricaturist next to him offered a few drawings of Defense Squad Z's members holding various trophies. The bootleg t-shirt vendor next to her sold shirts with pictures of Defense Squad Z labeled SQUAD GOALS.

"You know where Defense Squad Z is right now?" Monochrome asked the group.

Torpedo shrugged. "Probably getting another award?"

"Yes. Getting *yet another* award for saving Vignault's. An award that could have been ours if we hadn't acted like a bunch of jackasses."

"Leading by example," Brooks said.

"It seems like what you really want is an award," Cactus

Jack said.

"What I want is *good PR*. The kind an award brings."

"You could donate a bunch of money to orphans or something," Torpedo suggested.

Zane made a *pfft* noise. "That's not flashy. That's the sort of good PR that lasts hours. You have to give people something memorable. No one cares about orphans."

Well, that's true, Smith said, sulking about his childhood.

On the ground beneath the Wonder Wheel at Deno's Park, a crowd of Uggs-adorned visitors waited their turns, sipping over-priced and under-spiced pumpkin lattes. Like everything on Coney Island, the wheel creaked. It was no cause for alarm.

Then it creaked a little louder.

Then there was a loud SPRRREEEEEAK and the entire wheel made a violent, thirty-degree tilt toward the crowd. Room temperature latte rained on the crowd below as its members shrieked and dispersed.

The base of the wheel had come loose, and it rocked precariously above souvenir-strewn pavement. Soon the entire thing would fall on its side, severely injuring or killing its passengers.

As luck would have it, the Bedazzlers' walk had brought them to the area, and they rushed to the wheel when they heard the creak.

"Oh dear," Doctor Queer said, understating the problem.

"That's a class action waiting to happen," Cactus Jack said. "Can you telekinetically fix it?"

Doctor Queer's eyes shifted from side to side, avoiding eye contact. "...No."

"Come on," Blanche said. "That's gotta be something you can do."

"No. I'm afraid it's not," Doctor Queer lied. It was, but the cost was far too great.

"Well, let's see how strong this suit is," Torpedo said. She flew to the top of the wheel and gave it a push in the opposite direction of the tilt. It moved a few degrees. Then it snapped from its base, and she was the only thing keeping it in the air.

"Hey, Hot Stuff," Torpedo said. "How long can I hold this thing before it falls?"

"Twelve minutes," Hot Stuff said.

"Let's go, people!" Torpedo shouted.

Blanche crossed her arms. "Go where? None of us can freakin' fly."

"I can," Doctor Queer said. He handed Human Touch to Brooks and launched toward the sky with a "*momentum avem.*" He wasn't the only thing that launched, and it became apparent that the cost of flight was soiling himself.

"Gross," Human Touch said.

"It worked, though," Cactus Jack said. He watched as the magician began rescuing passengers, one by one, from the highest part of the wheel.

"I have an idea," Monochrome said.

"Oh *great*," Brooks said.

"Agitate me," Monochrome said.

Blanche scratched at her head. "What?"

"On it," Cactus Jack said as he turned to face Monochrome. "Your movies *suck*, dude."

The grounded team members surrounded their leader for an old-fashioned berating.

"I don't like working for Zane Industries," Human Touch said.

Cactus Jack agreed. "Nobody likes working for Zane Industries."

"You're not very nice," Blanche added.

Brooks stared Monochrome down. "You are the most aesthetically displeasing shade of grey *in the entire world*. The only way you could *ever* get someone to sleep with you is if they hated themselves."

You were supposed to insult him, Smith said.

"Well, that's true," Monochrome said, hands aglow. "Also, screw you."

He looked up at Torpedo and Doctor Queer and shouted "cool this!" as he shot magma toward each of the wheel's cars. Several riders buried their heads in their hands. Ducking and covering would work just as well against magma as it would against a nuclear strike, but they had to do *something*.

One dramatic rider belted, "We're all gonna die!"

Doctor Queer sighed and uttered "*glacies brrr.*" With a powder blue glow of his hands, he sent a cooling blast toward the magma. Then he caught hypothermia.

At the same time, Torpedo extinguished as much as she could from afar.

With the newly formed lava rock ramps, the non-aerial members of the team were able to run in and extract passengers. Brooks and Human Touch headed one direction, while Cactus Jack, Blanche, and Monochrome headed in others. Doctor Queer, shivering, continued his own efforts at the top of the wheel.

"Three minutes," Torpedo said, feeling the strain through her armor.

"We're all clear," Monochrome said.

Doctor Queer landed and bundled his arms, shivering.

"Everyone's out of the way?" Torpedo asked.

"Yup!" Blanche said.

Monochrome made a thin magma ring around Doctor Queer to warm him up.

"Thank you," Doctor Queer said.

"Hey, look at that." Monochrome said, impressed by his on-demand power. "You didn't even have to berate me."

Nobody was looking.

"I said 'hey, look at me—'" Monochrome cut off his catchphrase. "Fine."

Torpedo slowly decreased pressure on the wheel until she was on the ground. There was a problem with that, as the full weight of the wheel began driving her into the sidewalk.

"Little help here?" she asked.

Brooks handed Human Touch to Cactus Jack—she made a short noise of pain and protest—and ran toward the wheel to help prop it up.

Smith sassed him. *Are you trying to impress your date by winning the strongman game? Because if so, it's working.*

Torpedo jet-booted herself out of the ground but kept both hands on the wheel. "On the count of three?"

Brooks nodded.

On the count of three, they both jumped back and let the wheel fall its last few feet onto the ground with a modest THUMP. The pair walked back to the rest of the team, and Human Touch practically leapt from Cactus Jack's hand to Brooks's.

Monochrome spoke to the team. "That went well, I think."

The gathered crowd seemed to agree, as they broke into applause. Within minutes, #Bedazzlers and #ConeyIsland were trending on Twitter. It marked the first time the Bedazzlers had trended for a positive reason, and the first time Coney Island had trended at all.

"Can we get a picture with you guys?" a young girl asked on behalf of herself and her brother.

"Sure thing!" Blanche said.

"Here," the boy said, handing Blanche his cell phone.

Blanche took dozens of pictures of the rest of the team posing with the people they'd rescued as well as with random bystanders. The shots poured onto Instagram, and the team's approval rating was set to explode.

Then there was a noise even louder than the Wonder Wheel breaking. At first it sounded like a pack of motorcycles, and no one paid it any attention. When it continued for over a minute, getting louder and louder, and no motorcycles appeared, the crowd began to worry. Whispers of "what is that?" became loud utterances of "what *is* that?" and then became panicked shrieks of "WHAT THE FUCK IS THAT?" as a huge, unnatural shadow fell over the area.

For a moment, people feared that yet another rift in time and space had opened. The reality was less dire but equally distressing. Above the skyline appeared the slimy, olive-tone face of a gigantic sea monster.

12
SEA MINUS

T he sea monster that attacked Coney Island did not look like Cthulhu. It had no wings or feet, and had far more tentacles. It conveyed not the unknowable terrors of the deep, but the ickiness of a boneless cephalopod trying to keep itself upright on land. Under translucent skin, purple veins throbbed. Three stories above ground, at the top of its flopping body, sat a sunken head whose features were unnerving in their nearness to a human being's. It had sensitive eyes, a tiny bump where a person's nose would be, and a wide mouth.

"Ugh, it has teeth," Torpedo said.

"Yeah, this seems like it's in our wheelhouse," Brooks said.

"I disagree," Human Touch said, cowering behind him.

"I think we need to call the army," Cactus Jack said.

"Nonsense," Monochrome said. "It's a big puddle of jelly—how hard can it be to kill?"

Superheroes should never ask rhetorical questions. As the monster moved inland—dragging itself like a slug—buildings collapsed in its wake. There had never been a drill for evacuating during a sea monster attack, and it showed as crowds of people screamed and ran in every direction. A few tucked under a carousel, believing its metal roof to be a sturdy defense.

Monochrome, as usual, was cocky. "I've got this."

He bent his knees to brace himself, extended both arms,

and blasted magma at the creature as hard as he could. On impact, the magma turned to rock and crumbled to the ground.

The irritated creature brought one of its tentacles down on the carousel. Its metal roof collapsed, crushing dozens under the weight of colorful sheet metal and wooden horses.

Human Touch gasped. "This is horrible."

As if the creature could hear and wanted to spite her, it dropped another tentacle on a 24/7 walk-in clinic.

"Oh, *come on*," Cactus Jack said.

"We need to get its attention," Brooks said.

Monochrome yelled at it. "Sea monster! Hey!"

Nothing happened, but Monochrome couldn't accept that his plan of yelling at the creature wasn't a good one. "Maybe it's a Spanish-speaking sea monster."

"What?" Brooks said.

"Try yelling at it in Spanish," Monochrome said.

"I'm not yelling at a damned sea monster," Brooks said.

"You might as well," Cactus Jack said. "It might work, considering how everything has gone so far."

Brooks sighed. "*¡Monstruo marino! ¡Monstruo marino gigante!*"

Nothing happened.

"Maybe it's a kaiju," Monochrome said. "あなたはこ れ をしてはいけません、モンスター！"

Nothing happened.

"Does anyone on the team speak French?" Monochrome asked.

Torpedo had a different plan. She flew into action, darting around in the sky and hitting the creature with Zanium rays. They didn't seem to have any effect, but she kept trying.

"Hey!" ZAP! "Sea monster!" ZAP! "Hey!" ZAP!

The blasts didn't harm the creature, but they did keep it constrained to one sad, demolished amusement park. Torpedo circled its head, zapping and taunting to hold it in place.

Cactus Jack turned to Doctor Queer.

"Can you teleport it?" he asked.

"Only if I teleport myself as well," Doctor Queer said. "And that seems like a good way to be devoured by a sea monster."

"Or drown at the bottom of the ocean," Blanche said.

"HT," Monochrome said. "You wanna try that mind joo-joo on it?"

"No," Human Touch said.

Monochrome tilted his head. "*Will you anyway?*"

Human Touch sighed. "I guess."

Brooks ran with her to a nearby tentacle. They gave it a bear hug, and—thanks to Torpedo annoying it in the sky—the creature didn't seem to notice their presence. Human Touch, however, immediately felt its influence.

"I think my power works both ways," she said.

"What makes you say that?" Brooks asked.

"I have the sudden urge to kill people and eat krill."

"Yeah, let's not," Brooks said, pulling her from the tentacle with a SPLLIP.

"What happened?" Monochrome asked.

"It's just evil," Brooks said.

"Of course it is," Monochrome said.

"Its favorite color is blue," Human Touch said. "If that helps."

"Sure doesn't," Monochrome said.

There was a loud PLIPP and Monochrome jumped out of the way as Torpedo landed in the concrete where he'd been standing.

She pulled herself off the ground and dusted herself off. "It slapped me."

"Rebooting," Hot Stuff said.

"Any time would be great," Torpedo said.

Blanche stepped forward and motioned the others back with her hands. "Everyone close their eyes."

The other Bedazzlers obliged.

Blanche reached for her ski goggles and, with a dramatic gesture, pulled them from her eyes. A blinding light shot from her face toward the monster's. The creature squinted and roared, and she replaced the goggles.

"Okay," she said. "Open 'em."

It was effective, in that the sea monster was now blind. It was ineffective in that a blind sea monster was even more dangerous than a sea monster with sight.

The creature flailed wildly, fell sideways out of the amusement park, and took out several more buildings at once. A plume of dust and brine settled over the area, and the Bedazzlers shared a coughing fit.

"This just went from bad to worse," Monochrome said. "Thanks, Blanche."

"We know its eyes are penetrable now," Human Touch said. "Maybe we should focus our attacks there?"

Monochrome scoffed. "*Our* attacks? You don't do anything."

Torpedo ignored him. "I've been hitting the eyes. It isn't working." Then she saw something nobody else seemed to. "Jack, look out!"

Monochrome chastised her. "Codenames—"

A tentacle descended on Cactus Jack faster than he could move out of its way. He cowered to the ground and buried his head under his arms as the tentacle slammed into the ground. Everyone was certain they had just witnessed the black guy dying first, but when the monster screamed and raised its tentacle, Cactus Jack was fine. Better than fine, even. His entire body bristled with twelve-inch spines, and instead of retracting into his skin, several had embedded in the monster's tentacle. The creature retracted the appendage and brought it to its face to pick the spines out with its teeth.

As Jack stood, staring at his spiked arms in awe, a few spines ejected from his body, shot up, and hit the tentacle in the air. He shook himself off and the rest of the spines fell to the ground. For the first time in months, Jack appeared spine-free. He glanced down at his hand, thought hard, and made one emerge from his wrist at will.

"Human porcupine!" Monochrome shouted. "I knew it!"

"I am *not* the Human Porcupine," Cactus Jack said.

"Porcupines don't shoot their spines," Human Touch said.

"Or grow them at will," Torpedo said.

"Whatever," Monochrome said. "I'll have my people invent a porcupine that does."

"This gives me an idea," Cactus Jack said.

Brooks muttered under his breath, "You can't *invent* an animal, you jackass."

"The *other* God did," Monochrome said.

"Have you ever been diagnosed with narcissism?"

Monochrome laughed. "Why would I trust someone else's opinion of *me*?"

"System rebooted," Hot Stuff said.

Torpedo took that as her cue to fly up and resume zapping.

Cactus Jack turned to Doctor Queer. "Get me up there."

One "*momentum avem*" and a bowel evacuation later, Doctor Queer had carried Jack three stories up to the monster's face.

"What are you doing?" Torpedo asked between useless blasts.

"Next time he roars, throw me in," Jack said.

"What?" Doctor Queer asked. "That's a terrible idea."

"A really terrible idea," Torpedo agreed.

"Trust me," Cactus Jack said, despite the fact that he'd never done this before.

The creature roared, and Doctor Queer dropped Cactus Jack into its mouth. As soon as his feet hit its tongue, Cactus Jack turned himself into ball of spikes. The monster tried to swallow him, but his spiny body became lodged in the back of its throat.

"Oh my gosh," Blanche said.

In Brooks's mind, Smith snickered. *It can't swallow!*

Monochrome clapped his hands in glee. "It can't swallow!"

Joke retracted, Smith said.

The monster flailed harder than it had when Blanche blinded it. As it spun around trying to dislodge Jack from its throat, its tentacles grazed the ground, sending more dust and debris into the sky.

As Brooks yanked her away to evade some falling bricks, the elastic on Human Touch's mask snapped, revealing her face to the world. To her luck, no civilians could see anything but a brown haze.

When its death throes subsided, the monster's corpse fell to the ground, sending even more dust and squidgy bits of sea filth flying.

Brooks and Human Touch scurried over and pried open the creature's mouth. Jack walked out, covered in sea-liva but no worse for the wear. He expelled his spines to the ground.

"Your powers aren't useless!" Monochrome said. He looked at each member of the team. "Good job, everyone."

It sounded oddly sincere because it was. Each Bedazzler had played a role in rescuing the Wonder Wheel passengers and defeating the sea monster.

Cries of "help" and "oh God, my leg" alerted the team that their job wasn't done. Defense Squad Z's aid was contingent on the filing and approval of sixteen separate hardcopy forms.* In the meantime, there were hundreds of people trapped under rubble, and with first responders trapped behind walls of debris and sea scum, the Bedazzlers were the only emergency response on the scene.

For the next several hours, they toiled. Brooks and

---

* The forms were secured in manila file folders due to fear of a cyber attack, even though an actual attack was more likely, given the thousands of unhinged, powered superhumans running around.

Torpedo lifted broken pieces of buildings as Cactus Jack and Human Touch extracted people from the debris. In dark areas, Blanche ungloved her thumb and used the light it emitted to find survivors. Monochrome melted piles that were confirmed empty to get them out of the way and avoid duplicated effort. Doctor Queer used his *"remedium ululatus"* spell to heal the worst wounds, creating irritating papercuts on his own body in return.

In what was a turn for the team, New Yorkers were grateful. There were thanks, hugs, and even a few attempts at payment for their services, which they heroically refused. The news touted the team's success, and on-the-street interviews were universal in their praise for the Bedazzlers.

Then Monochrome took a disaster selfie.

13

OBLIGATORY INFIGHTING

After a teleport home in uncomfortable silence, the Bedazzlers sat in their common room in an even less comfortable silence. Monochrome's selfie had gone viral. In it, the Bedazzlers' leader could be seen grinning and roping a miserable, mask-free Human Touch into frame. In the background, Cactus Jack and Blanche assisted some of the sea monster's victims, but it wasn't enough to wash away the bad taste of the photo, in which there were visible corpses.

The public agreed that Godwin Zane was callous, at best. Worse, there were suggestions that he summoned the creature himself in order to defeat it and improve his PR. That this seemed to the media like something he would do bothered Zane a little. That his teammates wouldn't answer him bothered him a lot more. At least the media was giving him attention.

"Hello? I said 'what do you guys want for dinner—'"

The team ignored him, again.

Zane repeated himself. "What do you guys want—?"

Everyone broke the silence at once.

"For you to show some empathy," Abby said.

"A robot body for my husband," Brooks said.

"To benefit the world," Doctor Queer said.

"A new job," Jack said.

"A cure for my powers," Ana said.

"Tacos," Blanche said. "This poncho's been giving me

ideas."

Zane exhaled. "That's a lot to unpack. I can definitely do the tacos."

"What is wrong with you?" Abby asked.

"It wasn't *that* bad," Zane said.

"You took a disaster selfie!" Abby said.

Zane attempted a justification. "Defense Squad Z took selfies at Vignault's—"

"People asked them to," Jack said.

"There weren't dead and injured people in the background!" Abby said.

Zane threw up a finger. "Hang on." He walked to where Ana sat next to Doctor Queer and took her free hand.

Her lip curled. "What are you doing?"

"Getting a shot of empathy," Zane said.

"I don't think that's how it works," Ana said.

"It's not," Doctor Queer agreed. "I've done some research, and I believe Ana's ability to be some form of truth inducement. If the feeling isn't already under the surface, none would appear."

"He doesn't have *anything* under the surface," Brooks said.

He's got magma, Smith said.

Zane disputed the claim that he was empty. "I have dreams and ambitions and... stuff. I have lots of things. I have more things than you, probably."

"Yeah? How do you feel about that selfie?" Jack asked.

Zane shrugged. "I feel nothing."

"Nothing?" Abby asked.

"Nothing as far as that's concerned." His face became one of contemplation, and he let go of Ana's hand before he felt compelled to take the conversation down a different path.

Ana's eye twitched a little as he let go. She'd sensed something she hadn't had quite enough time to process.

Everyone was silent again, until they weren't.

"Yeah, so... I quit," Jack said.

"What?" Zane asked. "You can't quit. What about the bonus? There's no bonus until we get good PR."

"We're never going to get good PR with *you* around," Jack said. "I'll find some other way to get the money for my mom. This isn't worth it."

"I quit too," Abby said.

Zane threw his hands up. "What about the biography?"

"Oh, I have plenty of material now." She stood to exit.

Doctor Queer followed her lead and threw back his cape.

Ana, holding his hand, had no choice but to stand as well. "I have another internship offer that won't get me kicked out of the Criminal Justice program. And *it pays*."

"Arch?" Zane asked, somewhat hurt.

"As you know," Doctor Queer said, "I am compelled by oath to protect this dimension until I meet my end."

"Thank you," Zane said.

"But I've done that without aid for nearly two centuries."

"Come on," Zane said.

"I am your friend, Godwin, but I think you need some time alone to reflect. Perhaps my exit will hasten that."

"You guys. Seriously," Zane said. "It's not that bad. We almost got good PR this time."

"We don't care about PR," Abby said.

Zane shook his hands to keep them cool.

Abby offered a look of disgust. "Yeah. See? The fact that you're more worked up about PR than about disrespecting the dead or upsetting the team is exactly why we quit."

"If everyone else is gonna quit, I quit too," Blanche said.

"No one cares, Blanche," Zane said. He turned to Brooks. "You can't quit."

"I *can*," Brooks said. "I'm not going to because I need that robot, but there's no way I owe you more than the bare minimum. I'm going home, and you can call when you need my help."

Zane tried to pull one over on him. "I need your help."

"No. Seriously," Brooks said. "Someone had better be in danger."

"I'm in danger," Zane said.

Brooks rolled his eyes and headed for the seatrain.

"I'm in danger," Zane repeated.

"You will be if you keep harassing me," Brooks snipped.

With everyone else standing, Zane followed suit. "Guys. It's not that bad."

Jack stared at a message on his phone. "The nursing home wants to kick my mom out because the other residents are pestering her about her relation to the selfie guy."

"Well you should have worn a mask then," Zane said. "Come on. It's not *that* bad."

"Yeah, it's that bad," Abby said.

With that, she and the others boarded the seatrain to leave the Bedazzlestation for good. Zane tried to board with them, but Jack puffed his spikes out and blocked the door.

"Come on," Zane said as the doors shut.

On the other end, everyone went their separate ways: Jack and Brooks to Brooklyn, Abby and Ana to Queens, Doctor Queer to his Riverdale mansion in the Bronx, and Blanche— regrettably—to Staten Island.

14

THE D IN DATE

Most of the Bedazzlers' journeys home were uneventful. Abby's was the least so. She walked through Queens with Ana, trying to reassure the younger woman that her parents would not murder her.

"I can't believe the mask came off," Abby said. "You should sue the party store."

Ana shrugged. "It's my fault. I went to the 99 Cent Shoppe so I could pocket the other nine dollars."

"Is your family that poor, or—"

"I told them I received a lot more scholarship money than I did. So they don't think I need help."

"Well, why would you lie about that?" Abby asked.

"Because I could," Ana said. She lowered her head. "I don't get to rebel much."

"Well, you pulled off the ultimate rebellion this time. You're internet famous."

Ana shook her head. "I'm going to get kicked out of my program, and they're actually going to kill me."

"But you've got that other internship lined up, right?"

"Yeah, that was a lie too."

"Well, you're really good at lying." Abby came to both a stop and a realization. "So Depeche Mode..."

"Who hasn't heard of Depeche Mode?" Ana laughed.

"You just wanted to get a rise out of Zane?" Abby asked.

Ana answered emotionlessly. "I didn't know what would

happen."

"Heyyyyyyyyyyy," a voice said from behind them.

The two women instantly recognized the sound of a drunk man whose flirting, when rejected, would turn to aggression.

"Oh, great," Abby said.

True to type, the man hurried around the women to meet them head on. His breath smelled of whiskey and, for some reason, carrot cake.

"Issa lovely evening, innit?" He was slurring, not British.

Ana tensed up. "Yeah..."

"Wassamatter?" He looked down to where the women held hands and frowned. "Ohwasee how it isss. I betchu two's never had a reeeeal mannn."

"I don't know about her, but I've had *plenty*," Abby said. "Can't write erotica without doing the research."

Ana's eyes went wide. "What are you doing?"

Standard protocol is to smile and brush off compliments until reaching a well-lit area, but Abby had just helped defeat a sea monster, and she spoke with confidence.

"We're not interested. Go away."

"Bitch." The drunk forced his arm between them, pushed Ana aside, and ran his hand up Abby's arm to her shoulder. "I can setcher attitude straight."

Ana, alone on the sidewalk, let out a series of gasps.

"I don't like fighting—" Abby said.

"Attagirl."

She landed her boot right between his legs. "—but here we are."

The drunk doubled over and puked on the sidewalk.

Abby reached down for Ana's hand and pulled her along. They ran until the coast was clear.

"Are you okay?" Abby asked.

Ana nodded. "I'm fine."

"Is that a lie?" Abby asked.

Ana answered with a nervous chuckle. "No..."

"That was dumb," Abby said. "I shouldn't have confronted him, what with your power. I just... I had enough of drunken assholes growing up, and if I could fight a sea monster, I figured I could—"

"It's fine," Ana said. "We lived."

"Sorry you're not going to find your cure," Abby said.

"Oh, I don't know about that." Ana readied a single air quote. "'Doctor Queer' is still researching it for me."

"Still?"

"Yeah, apparently that mind control command didn't wear off. He keeps texting me updates. And for an old guy, he uses *a lot* of emojis."

"You're kidding," Abby said.

"Look," Ana said.

She pulled out a text message:

> ●●●● Look at this. 👉 "Empathic
> Projection or Emotion Augmentation?
> A Study in Super-Sensitivity" by Herb
> Honeycutt, m.articles.magesearch.net/
> 1971/08/15/.../.../honeycutt/index.htm?
> source=facebook 😊😊😊😊😊 I think you
> may find this useful ⚔ 🏹 We march 🚶 🏃
> ever closer to finding the key 🔑 to power
> suppression. 🍕

Abby laughed. "Why did he include the pizza?"

"No idea. You should see how often he uses the eggplant."

"You *know* he calls it an aubergine." Abby waved her free hand around in her best Doctor Queer impression. Her voice boomed. "It was only six fortnights ago that an aubergine was essential in stopping the evil Cecil from collapsing the foundations of Earth Fourteen!"

Ana spoke between chuckles. "That's my house."

It was a narrow, green home that looked far too picture

perfect. Not one brick of its staircase was chipped or out of place, and the porch light didn't flicker.

Abby ignored the unnervingly pristine home and spoke with sincerity. "Hey, you're only a few blocks away from me. The Bedazzlers may have been a bust, but let me know if you ever want to hang out with someone who's dealt with... weirdness."

"You can come in if you want," Ana said, hopeful.

"Oh, no. I am *not* into family drama. I'm handing you off and getting out of here."

"Fair enough," Ana said.

At the top of the staircase, the front door flung open before Ana could slide her key into the lock. Ana's mother greeted her, wearing moon and star pajamas and a forced smile.

"Ana." Mrs. Nakamura shook her head. "And...?"

True to her word, Abby pushed Ana at her mom's hand and backed down the stairs. "Abby Waters. Sorry, but I have an appointment."

"After midnight?" Mrs. Nakamura asked.

Abby waved. "Yep!"

It was true, in a way. She had an appointment with her keyboard and a sexy he-wolf named Rafael. Abby fled and didn't look back.

Abby wasn't the first ex-Bedazzler to arrive at her apartment complex. As she closed in, she could tell. Peter Gabriel's "In Your Eyes" played at an unacceptable volume for one o'clock in the morning, and there was the occasional shout of "Turn it off!" from an upstairs window. The source of the latter was her disgruntled neighbor. The source of the former was Godwin Zane, parked in a lawn chair holding a portable

Zanetooth speaker.

She walked up behind him and tapped him on the shoulder. "What are you doing here?"

"Oh. You're not inside," he said. He casually hopped off the chair and stood to face her. "I've been trying to lure you out for an hour."

"With Peter Gabriel?" Abby said. "That's horrible."

Zane shrugged, and Peter Gabriel kept singing. "I'm ready to give you that interview."

She raised her brow. "1994?"

He nodded. "1994."

"Why now?" she asked in suspicion.

"I'm interested in you," Zane said. "Sexually."

"Yeah, I know. You've made that abundantly clear."

Zane put a hand to his chin. "Have I?"

"With the armor and trying to be my date and constantly saying how you're into black women? Yeah. Crystal."

"Well, there's no team and I wanted to see you again, so I'll do the interview," Zane said.

"I feel like there *has* to be a catch," Abby said.

Zane shrugged. "I'll do it after you go on a date with me."

Abby groaned. "Ohhh. No."

"Turn it off!" the upstairs voice shouted again.

"No!" Zane shouted back. "Peter Gabriel adds ambience! It's essential!"

"Turn it off," Abby said.

"Did you not hear what I just said? It's adding ambience."

Abby rubbed at her temples. "For whom?"

"For you."

"But I just told you to turn it off."

Zane groaned and tapped a button on his phone to silence Peter Gabriel. "Women are so complicated."

Abby stared at him. "I told you *exactly* what I wanted you to do."

"And it was complicated."

"*Oh my God.*"

He smiled at her. "Yes?"

She smacked herself in the forehead. "Not *you.*"

"So, what do you say?" Zane asked.

Two sides of her mind debated with an intensity normally reserved for those who enjoy ranting about the lizard takeover of America. On one hand, she'd already agreed to don a suit of armor and risk her life fighting crime with Zanium rays in order to get a juicy scoop. On the other hand, going on a date with Godwin Zane was almost certain to be worse.

She sought more information. "What kind of date?"

"The sky's the limit," Zane said. "Actually, it's not. I have a spaceship."

"Can it be normal?" she asked.

He leaned in. "What do you mean?"

"If I just go to dinner with you, will that count?"

Zane chuckled. "Well, that wouldn't be a date at all, would it?"

"Yes, it would," Abby said.

"We have to at least go bog snorkeling," Zane said.

Her dignity beat out her curiosity, and Abby walked toward the building's front door. "Pass."

Zane followed her up the steps with another suggestion. "Cheese rolling?"

"No."

"Diamond caking?"

She turned back and looked him in the eyes. "I don't even want to know what that is."

"It's—"

The door shut in his face, and Zane crossed his arms and bit his lip. He didn't have a drawing board, but it was time to buy one so he could go back to it.

15

SOLO ADVENTURES

At 55 Decatur Street in Brooklyn, Brooks was welcomed home by two teenagers: Patience, a former Puritan from the 1690s, and Lemon, a hipster from the 2200s.* They hadn't seen him in four days, so when he came through the door, they abandoned movie night and swarmed him for a group hug.

"Mr. Brooks!" Patience said, ever formal.

"Turo!" Lemon said, ever not.

"Hey," he said. "You two doing okay?"

The girls nodded.

"You haven't gotten into trouble with vampires or anything?" he asked.

"Nope." Lemon motioned toward her violin, sitting on the coffee table. "I've mostly been practicing with the band."

Pop Tart & the Activation Energy were never going to hit it big and, being from the future, Lemon knew that. But their music still needed to be made. She had things to say—important things like "don't date guys named Duke."

Patience, meanwhile, had begun her junior year of high school.

"I was asked to attend homecoming," she said.

"Really? That's great," Brooks said.

———————————————

* It's a whole thing. Move past it.

"I declined, of course," Patience said. Her birth father had been an avid dance opponent. Though he'd once had her hanged as a witch and she tried to distance herself from his views, a Puritan disapproval of dancing was still ingrained in her mind and wouldn't shake loose.

"Of course," Brooks said.

"How is Mr. Zane?" Patience asked. She was Godwin Zane's number one fan, and she used her passion for him to replace her lapsed passion for God punishing the wicked. It took her months to figure out how to make a rudimentary fansite with a Wix template, but it was up to six views per day. Someday, she hoped, Brooks would ask her to join him for Take Your Daughter to Work Day.

"Uh, he's fine," Brooks assured her.

"Is this another drive-by?" Lemon asked. "Or are you gonna stick around for a while?"

Brooks opened a closet and hung his coat. "I'm going to stick around forever. The Bedazzlers are done."

Patience frowned a polite frown that read as a neutral face.

Lemon speculated. "Because of the selfie?"

Brooks nodded.

"That sucks. Are you still gonna get a body for Eddie?"

Tell them I said 'hi.'

"I don't know," Brooks said. "But he says 'hi.'"

Lemon scoffed. "I'm still not speaking to him."

She says she's not speaking to—

I know. I'm in your head. How long is she going to—

"He wants to know how long you're going to stay mad at him," Brooks said.

Lemon crossed her arms. "Until he gets a body and I can berate him myself."

Brooks eyed the popcorn. "So what are you watching?"

Patience frowned harder than before, this time almost making her displeasure known. "*The Crucible*. It's quite inaccurate."

Brooks laughed. "The one with Daniel Day-Lewis?"

"No," Lemon said. "There's a low budget Canadian version that basically nobody has seen. It's perfect."

"Mind if I watch it with you?" he asked.

"Be our guest," Lemon said.

He took a seat between the two girls and settled in for the worst thing he'd seen since Coney Island was destroyed by a sea monster.

She deserves better than this.

That's what Jack thought every time he visited his mother. There wasn't anything wrong with Cedar Acres, but there wasn't anything right about it either. It was soulless. Patients were taken care of. They were fed, medicated, and groomed when necessary. BINGO happened every Thursday, and reruns of *I Love Lucy* aired every day. But the place lacked heart. It was a budget senior care facility, and it afforded budget amenities. The staff's indifference was its own cruelty.

He tried to spruce her room up with potted plants, but she could never remember to water them, and the staff wasn't paid to do that. So the plants died. While his mother slept, he replaced some dead violets with living ones. The sound of the pot touching the bedside table was too loud, and Jack froze, hoping it hadn't awakened her. As he stood perfectly still, watching for any rustling, he noticed that the sheets were stained, and he frowned.

He went to law school, and felt he should have been able to afford better for her. But one circumstance had led to another and he'd ended up in a bottom-tier school that afforded bottom-tier opportunities like the one at Zane Industries. Rent wasn't cheap. Alimony wasn't any cheaper.

Lorraine awoke with a series of slow blinks.

"Jack?" she wondered. "Did you shave your beard?"

He'd never had a beard in his life. This, at least, was an understandable mistake, since his bone spines had previously given the appearance of scruffy white facial hair. Her next mistake was not as understandable.

"Where are the children?" she asked.

He wished she hadn't woken up and wished he didn't feel guilty about the first wish. "We never had any, Mom."

"Where's Lysa?"

"We split five years ago, Mom."

"When's Marcus going to come by again?"

His brother had died ten years earlier, but he couldn't break the news to her again.

"Soon, Mom," he assured her.

An orderly, summoned by the sound of conversation, stood in the doorway.

He chastised Jack. "You're not supposed to be here."

"I was just leaving," Jack said.

"*You're not supposed to be here*," the orderly repeated.

As Jack maneuvered by him and through the doorway, he scolded the man. "I'm not going to abandon my mom."

"Well you're not going to see her at Cedar Acres."

"I sure hope not," Jack said.

Ana raged at her parents for not making any sense. Well, she raged on the inside, and for good reason: they'd grounded her. She was twenty-one years old and they'd grounded her. It shouldn't have even been possible. One day she was gallivanting around town trying to make an emotional connection with a sea monster, the next she was lying in bed holding hands with her mother, forbidden from leaving the house.

"Your father should have the stew ready any minute," her

mother said.

Ana didn't respond, preferring *to* stew.

There was a gentle tap at her bedroom door. Too gentle to be her father's.

"Come in," Ana droned.

"You're not supposed to have any visitors," Mrs. Naka-mura said as a young woman entered. She changed her mind when she realized it was Teresa, recovered from food poi-soning and ready to take Ana off her hands. "Never mind. This is perfect. I'll be downstairs helping with dessert."

Interns are not paid enough to have assistants. At Zane Industries, they weren't paid at all. But Ana's parents be-lieved their daughter to be the exceptional exception, so they didn't question it. Plus, she was a fantastic liar.

"I tried to visit the hospital, but I couldn't get the room number," Ana said. She pulled Teresa in for a hug that ended quickly.

Teresa still looked sick. Her short, wavy brown hair was matted to her head in a way that said she'd been sweating hard—the way hair looks when a person has been puking for a few hours straight.

Ana noticed and didn't understand the visit. "You're feel-ing better?"

Teresa moved her head in a way that was halfway between a shake and a nod.

Ana was confused. "No?"

"I didn't have food poisoning," Teresa said.

"Oh." Ana had a feeling about what that meant. "*Oh.*"

"Every time we hold hands, I feel like I have to tell you the truth. I wasn't ready to do that, so I had to get away for a few days."

Ana had a good feeling what the truth was, but she asked anyway. "What—"

"I want to break up," Teresa said.

It was exactly what she expected. "Is it the hand thing?

Because Mr. Zane has it in his queue—"

"A little bit," Teresa said. "Mostly it's pretending to be your assistant. All the lying."

"Is there any way I can change your mind?" Ana asked.

"No. Not really."

After a few minutes spent in silence, they made an uncomfortable descent down the stairs, hand-in-hand, and approached Ana's mother.

"Mom, I need your hand," Ana said.

"Why's that?"

"Teresa got a new job," she said. "She's not going to be my assistant anymore."

"Oh, I'm sorry to hear that," her mother said. Then she did something awful. "Would you like to stay for dinner one last time?"

Teresa did not, but she couldn't refuse.

They settled in for something even more uncomfortable than the disaster selfie.

Quiet.

The first step in meditation using the Q.U.E.E.R. Method was finding a place that afforded complete silence. Reflection, Doctor Queer always said, could only occur in a bubble. In this case, it was literally a bubble, as the quiet spot Godwin Zane found was the empty Bedazzlestation. He hopped onto a table in the cafeteria, sat cross-legged, and began thinking about himself. That part came easy.

Unhappiness.

The next step was identifying the one or more things that made the meditator unhappy about their lot in life. For Zane, it was seeing everything he'd worked for fall apart through no fault of his own. His company was about to go under.

The Bedazzlers had already gone under. He was thirty-three, and his white hair was beginning to grey. It made no sense, but it was happening. Doug Daniels was a person who existed—stupid, alliterative name and all. Zane tallied up a list of grievances in his mind and fixated on the most irritating of all: Abby's refusal to go on a date with him.

Exoneration.

The third step was where Zane's meditation always went south. Exoneration was meant for the meditator to forgive everything they'd done wrong. As it was impossible for Zane to believe he'd done wrong, he could never make this work. Everything around him kept failing, though, so he searched and searched for something he could improve. Something that was the source of at least two of his grievances.

The selfie, he thought. *I shouldn't have taken the selfie, but I forgive myself for doing it.*

Empowerment.

The fourth step was not literal empowerment, as he could shoot magma from his hands. It was about seeing what he could do to change his circumstances and resolving to do that thing.

How can I get them back here? He thought. *I could bribe them. No. Yes. No...*

Thinking was hard.

I owned my mistake. I wonder if...

It hit him. *I need to publicly apologize.*

Release.

Doctor Queer never advocated this step, but Zane didn't like the look of the Q.U.E.E. Method, so he tacked sexual release to the end of it. He grabbed his phone, pulled up SexyPuddingCupHentai.com, and got to work.

It wasn't sexy enough. No matter how many times Abby re-wrote the paragraph, it wasn't sexy enough.

> The wolf-man howled hard at the rising moon. Tonight was his last chance, or it would be another thirty days. He needed to lie with Triana tonight. He pounded at his chest, amping himself up for the transformation and pursuit. His masculine, hairy legs began shrinking into small, furry ones. His fingers twisted into paws. His entire body compressed itself into a smaller form while his skull lengthened. His senses heightened. The frigid air no longer made his nipples hard. Instead, it made his tail wag.

She pressed the backspace key until the entire paragraph was gone. She could have selected and deleted it in bulk, but the repeated tapping made her edits feel more brutal. And boy did her edits deserve to be brutal. Even after a few hours on the phone with Brooks's shapeshifter friend, she couldn't put the feeling of a transformation to paper. After deleting the sixteenth iteration of the wolf-man's transformation, she switched windows and scanned the biography-in-progress.

> Interacting with Godwin Zane is like interacting with a force of nature. He doesn't converse with you; he throws whatever he wants at you. In my months of observation, I've walked in on him juggling, shouting at a goldfish, and trying to turn off a television with his mind. That last one was part of a product test, but I wouldn't have been surprised if it hadn't been.

> Zane suffers a terrible loneliness, and while he's enough of a narcissist that it doesn't bother him, I have seen brief flickers of humanity. I once told him that I was homeschooled, aware that was something we had in common. I expected to hear a few stories about his upbringing, of course. I didn't expect the way he

enthusiastically shouted "me too!" It was clear he wanted to make a connection, but it just wasn't possible. He ended up going off onto some tangent about giraffes that day.

There's a tragedy there. Zane doesn't surround himself with sycophants. His behavior can't be excused because everyone around him tells him "yes." They don't. He genuinely has no understanding of how to be a person.

Abby stared at her screen and frowned.

Every October, Doctor Queer visited Arkansas. Because he'd been wrapped up with the Bedazzlers, this year's visit was a few weeks overdue. He teleported himself to a barren field where no one would notice his hours-long paralysis. When he came to, everything was just as he'd left it. It usually was. Once, in 1987, a group of teens had smashed beer bottles on the stones, but that was an aberration.

It was his property—given to him by President John Tyler—and he'd visited every year since 1844. That was the year he'd buried Ambrosia, and forty years later he'd done the same for Jane. There was little time in his life for family, but he took one day a year to remember the only one he'd ever had. There were no gravestones. Instead, stone piles marked each year that had passed: 170 for Ambrosia and 130 for Jane. The piles were growing large. He reached under his cloak and pulled out two rocks, then knelt down and added one to each pile.

"Another year has passed," he said. "For now, my fight continues. Know that I haven't forgotten either of you, and that I press on in your memory so the world which created you is not lost."

He turned and let out an anguished sigh.

A rude chuckle came from behind his back.

The doctor turned to find himself face-to-face with the dread Percival. The sorcerer was a perfect evil mirror for Doctor Queer. He wore an elaborate gold cloak with silver trim over a black speedo and leather boots. His skin was reddish purple, a product of being from another dimension and a different species, but it didn't detract from his go-ahead-and-eat-the-forbidden-fruit style of charm.

"I came here to kill you," Percival said.

"I'm afraid I'm not in the mood for one of our fights right now," Doctor Queer said.

"No kidding." Percival noted his rival's damp eyes—eyes that took the fun right out of defeating the Divine Dimensionmaster. "I didn't know you had a family."

"Why would you?" Doctor Queer asked.

"It simply... never occurred to me," Percival said.

In order to put his best divine, dimensionmastering foot forward, Doctor Queer wiped an uncomfortable tear from his face and puffed out his chest. He tossed the cloak that had fallen in front of him back over his shoulder and entered his normal spellcasting stance.

"I have defeated you before, and I shall do it again," Doctor Queer said.

Percival was bummed out. "I don't know. I'm not really up for this anymore. Can I buy you a drink?"

"Excuse me?"

"Let me buy you a drink," Percival said.

Butternut was blind, but that didn't stop the ginger cat from strutting around like he owned the place. The first victim of Blanche's powers didn't hold his disability against her, and when she arrived home for the first time in almost a week, the tomcat weaved between her legs, purring.

"Hey, Butternut!" she said. "You want a treat? I betcha do!"

It was a testament to Staten Island's shittiness that Blanche was able to buy a thousand-square-foot cottage there on only her income. But she had, and she was finally alone. She threw off the poncho, winter coat, and the rest of her outdoor clothing and breathed a sigh of relief that only lounging around in undergarments could bring. Then she grabbed Butternut's treat bag and gave it a shake. Without sight, the cat's hearing was even better than the average feline's, and he yelped a short, happy meow so she would deliver the treats to the floor beneath him.

With Butternut's hunger squashed, Blanche plopped onto the couch and pulled a brown crocheted blanket over herself. Butternut hopped up next to her and nestled in to listen to *Wheel of Fortune.*

She settled in and began knitting him a Halloween sweater.

16

ESCALATION

Monochrome took the stage with a heavy cape and a heavy heart. *Sergei & Tina*, the nation's top-rated early morning talk show, was the sort of program that people like Blanche—middle-aged, midwestern, and generally middling—watched. The live studio audience was filled with Blanches, each familiar with knitting needles, cats, and perpetual singledom.

A "fun" thing about *Sergei & Tina* was that all four guests were brought out at the beginning of the hour-long show. They had to sit and politely applaud each other's interviews and demonstrations, no matter how much their minds disagreed with the praise. Zane was slated to speak with the hosts last, and so he sat on the far end of a purple couch, forcing his hands together to welcome a fourth-grade class's rendition of "All About That Bass." It was an out-of-date song, and the lyrics had been changed to be kid-friendly. The children warbled off-key, with some a few beats behind the rest:

> *Yeah it's pretty clear, I ain't no age two*
> *But I can do math homework, like I'm supposed to do*
> *'Cause I got that boom boom that all the teachers praise*
> *All of my nouns are in all the right cases*

Zane distracted himself by counting the audience members he'd be willing to sleep with. The number was six in a crowd of two hundred. For some reason, the kids still weren't done when his count was, so he filed a recount with his own authority. The second poll came up with five bangables.

Who am I kidding? he thought. *If I could, I'd bang any of them.*

The singing came to a stop and boisterous applause came to a start. He caught on just in time to make things awkward, as his claps began just as everyone else's ended.

"Great job?" he said.

Tina's head bobbed up and down. "It sure was!"

"Up next," Sergei said, "we'll have a cooking demonstration with R.J. Fillenputty. Stay tuned."

The crowd could hardly contain itself during commercial break as a turtleneck-clad crew brought out a demo station complete with a cooktop and bowls upon bowls of fresh vegetables and spices. Audience members murmured, knowing they were in for a treat.[*]

No one on stage shared their enthusiasm. As the guests shuffled their hands and feet in silence, Sergei smoked a cigarette, and Tina fiddled with her phone. The hosts hated each other, and it showed. Their cheer turned on when the cameras did.

"And we're back!" Tina said.

Sergei raised his arms toward the audience. "Are you all ready to make some tacos?"

They were, and they cheered.

R.J. Fillenputty (pronunciation: fi ɪnˈpʌti) was the energetic, food-obsessed host of *Restaurants, Restaurants, and Restaurants*. He jumped up from the couch and ran to the demo station, pumping his fists while shouting "come on!" and "yeah!"

As the audience went batshit insane with applause and screams, Zane pondered. His company had, despite a few

---

* Figuratively. No show will feed its audience due to liability.

setbacks, given the world some amazing advances in technology. Yet he had been welcomed to the room with boos while everyone loved the spiky-haired douchebag making braised pork tacos in front of him. A moment of self-reflection tapped at the front of his mind, but he spurned it like a door-to-door salesman. Instead of considering his own actions, he considered whether he should start a cooking show. After all, it had worked well enough for R.J., and there was no show currently on the air that featured a host cooking with magma.

Before long, the demo was finished.

"That's a taco!" the chef shouted. He clapped to his own words. "That. Is. A. Taco!"

The audience seemed to agree, and they cheered some more.

"Thank you, R.J.!" Sergei said.

Tina pointed to a stain on his apron. "You've got a little something—"

R.J. scraped a dab of sauce off his apron and brought it to his mouth. "Not anymore, I don't!"

The three shared a laugh with the audience.

When the show returned from yet another silent commercial break, Zane clapped along to the tune of "I Wish You Were All Dead," a song he'd just conceived in his mind. It was a peppy New Wave number with a fantastic synth hook that he forgot as soon as the third guest stood for her interview.

Cecily Dade was an A-list celebrity for reasons that had nothing to do with her acting ability. She was the six-time Sexiest Woman Alive, as voted by Nubbin Magazine, and nine-time Teen Choice Award winner in such categories as "Hottest Face," "Hottest Abs," and "Hottest Scene That Took Place on a Boat." She also had several issues that demanded intervention. A few weeks prior to her appearance on *Sergei & Tina*, Cecily had driven her luxury SUV intoxicated and backed over an entire class of preschoolers. Two died. You wouldn't know it from her cheery saunter over to the stool between Sergei and Tina.

"So you're out of rehab," Sergei said.

Cecily nodded. "I really learned a lot in those three days."

"Such as?" Sergei asked.

"How to get out of rehab in three days," Cecily said.

The hosts chuckled.

"Let's talk about cheerier things," Tina said. "*Gatortopia: Dawn of the Gators.*"

Cecily smiled wide. "Yeah, so... it's a prequel to *Gatortopia* and *Gatortopia 2: the Gatoring...*"

"Now hold on," Sergei said, feigning ignorance for the crowd's amusement. "It's the third movie, but it takes place before the other two movies?"

"That's right," Cecily said.

"But you're older than you were in those movies," Tina said.

"She doesn't look it," Sergei said with a wink.

Cecily made an oh-stop-it gesture, and the three of them giggled.

Well, at least they're lobbing nothing but softballs, Zane thought.

There was some talk of *Gatortopia 4*, a thrilling conversation about Cecily's forthcoming fashion line, and a foray into the world of engagement chatter. Every moment of it was terrible, and Zane only survived by imagining himself being heaped with praise at the end of his own interview.

Two commercial breaks later, it was time.

"You know our next guest from the *Look at Me!* film series, as well as from being the CEO of Zane Industries and—most recently—leader of the Bedazzlers. Please welcome... Godwin Zane... also known as... Monochrome!"

Zane had beautiful, humble words prepared, and the crowd booed him as he approached the interview stool to speak them. He found that both strange and annoying.

Tina pressed her hands down at the air to direct the crowd to stop. "All right, all right."

"Mr. Zane," Sergei said.

Tina nodded. "Or Monochrome... do you have a preference?"

Zane shrugged. "Either is fine."

Sergei pulled out a printed copy of the disaster selfie photo and held it up for the camera. "Let's get right to it. This viral photo."

The audience booed again.

"Yes," Zane said. "Um. That is me, and I did take a selfie there."

The audience booed harder.

Zane held up a shushing hand. "Yeah, I know."

"Well, don't shush them," Sergei said. "This is a free-speech zone."

Zane squinted. "I'm not. I'm acknowledging that they're right to boo. I took the selfie."

"While New Yorkers were injured and dying in the background?" Tina asked.

"Yes," Zane said.

The boos grew louder.

"I know. I know." Zane said. "That's why I'm here. To apologize for my behavior."

"Are you *really* sorry?" Tina asked.

"I am," Zane said. It wasn't a total lie, as he was sorry the incident had affected him negatively. "Like many, I can get so caught up in documenting my life that I lose my sense of when it's appropriate."

Sergei nodded. "I think a lot of people can relate to that."

"People expect better from me, and they should. I expect better from myself."

"That's very mature," Tina said. "Can your fans expect to see more of this thoughtful version of Monochrome?"

"Well, they can't expect to see me at all. Zane Industries

will be clo—"

"Hang on," Sergei said. "I'm told we have an incoming message for you."

Zane offered a puzzled look. "What? Who does that?"

The hosts, without a script, sat silent with their exaggerated made-for-TV smiles. They didn't say anything as monitors in the studio played a message for both Zane and the viewers at home.

It was a touch overstated. Dramatic bass bursts punctuated distorted drum ticks in a sound reminiscent of every movie trailer ever. A male face appeared with just enough lighting to see his lips move but not enough to make out any distinguishing features. His voice had been adjusted to be deep and unnerving.

"This is a message for Monochrome," he said.

The audience booed.

Zane crossed his arms. "Oh, for crying out loud—"

"I have your friends," the face said.

Zane thought that was odd, as he had none.

The voice continued. "I want the Bedazzlers! If you don't meet me at the Coney Island rubble by noon, people you care about will die."

"There are no Bedazzlers," Zane said. "The team—"

"It's not a two-way message," Tina said.

"Yes it is. You're broadcasting what I'm saying. The team is done. My company is done."

There was a rousing BOOOOOOOOOOOOOO.

Zane hopped up and confronted the crowd with outstretched arms. "You hate me, and I just told you I quit. Why are you booing now?"

They didn't appreciate the confrontation and responded with a louder BOOOOOOOOOOOOOOOOOOOOOOOO.

He gestured back toward the couch at R.J. "That guy has eight divorces under his belt!" He pointed at Cecily. "She mowed over children!" He jerked his head toward Mrs.

Troxell, who was responsible for the off-key fourth grade class. "She should have mowed *her students* over!"

BOOOOOOOOOOOOOOOOOOOOOOOOOOOOOOO OOOOOOOOOOOOOOO!

"This doesn't seem like a new, thoughtful Monochrome at all," Sergei said.

"You two are supposed to ask about movies and fashion and keep it light," Zane said. "Ask me about *Look at Me! 10* or something."

Tina shook her head. "When will you change, Godwin?"

"I don't need to—" His hands beginning to glow, he cut himself off for PR purposes and stared at the audience. "I'll go meet this guy and save people, okay? Is that what you want?"

The crowd stopped booing.

"I'll go save the world or whatever. Are you happy?"

The hosts nodded, and the audience murmured in mild agreement.

"Really?" Zane asked. "I can't do better than a pork taco?"

In lieu of boos, the crowd surrendered a polite clap. The applause at a Randy Newman concert would have been stronger, but at least this was applause. Monochrome strolled offstage to it, giving his hands a cooling shake the whole way.

One of Jack Cashmere's deepest secrets was that he loved watching *Sergei & Tina*. He called Blanche to alert her to what had happened so she could alert the others, allowing him to keep his secret safe. She was already watching the show, and she started making some calls.

17

CATCHING MONO

Monochrome, fully costumed and fully agitated, headed for Coney Island, alone. He had arrived well before noon, but the evil TV face hadn't specified where he should meet it, so he wandered around blocks upon blocks of smoldering ruin for over two hours. Eventually, he made it to an area that was still intact but abandoned on account of the nearby destruction. The quiet walk there would have been a great time for self-reflection, if Godwin Zane were one for reflecting.

What am I even looking for?

He was about to give up when he rounded a corner and found the answer: a standard model warehouse, indistinguishable from those that bordered it. Well, indistinguishable but for the costumed corpse strung up across an open garage door. The Horse Whisperer, one of Defense Squad Z's finest, hung spread out in an X with several stab wounds and the words NO HEROES finger-painted on his bare chest with blood.

"Yikes," Monochrome said, slightly bothered. He stepped away and tapped at his chin.

Actual murder seems a bit extreme, he thought. *I should call the police. But then again... If the rest of Defense Squad Z are in there and I save them, I'll definitely win a medal and save Zane Industries. And the Bedazzlers will have no choice but to recognize that I'm a super-hero...a way better one than any of them. And Abby will find me irresistible. On the other hand, if this guy killed Defense Squad Z, he'll probably be able to kill me, and I definitely don't want to die... Yeah, I'm going to call the police.*

He did, but it didn't go as well as he'd hoped. An annoyed dispatcher promised him that, despite several calls expressing concern about Horse Whisperer's dead body, the building's owner had assured them it was nothing more than a Halloween decoration.

"I feel like you should come check," Monochrome said. "Because this is definitely a dead body."

"Sir, the NYPD does not need your advice on how to do its job."

A dial tone let him know he'd been hung up on.

"Sigh," he said to himself. He put his Zanephone into front-facing camera mode and inspected his outfit. Thanks to a stiff breeze, the cape needed a minor adjustment to look its best, so he shimmied it into place. Down to half a dozen sponsors, the abundance of ad-less space made him frown. Eyeing that frown, he realized his skin looked a little washed out, so he pulled a custom greytone compact from his pocket and gave his face a dusting. Then there was the ritual of making sure every hair on his head was in the right place and plucking the one grey hair among the white. All told, this superheroing beauty routine took about sixteen minutes. Only when he was presentable was it time to enter the warehouse.

At the back of the garage was an open steel door. Through that lay an expanse of wooden crates. Formerly the home of an innocent illegal drug enterprise, the warehouse was now home to a superhero-killing enterprise. Under bright spotlights, it became clear that the Horse Whisperer had not been the only casualty.

Scattered across one crate lay the hacked-apart pieces of Great Aim. Sprawled across another lay Laser Scream, her mouth still gaping from her last scream. Slumped over yet another was the mangled body of The Law.

Monochrome couldn't help but chuckle to himself. "Looks like someone fought The Law, and The Law lost."

Steel Foot and Admiral Milky Way were also dead, their bloodied corpses contorted together in a failed, last-ditch effort to enact the Milky Foot combination maneuver.

"This is your fault." The TV voice echoed through the warehouse.

Not sure where to aim his face, Monochrome looked up at the ceiling. "How?"

"You're late. I told you to be here by noon or people would die."

"You didn't give me an address! I think I made it here in impressive time, all things considered," Monochrome said.

"Oh, well," the voice said. "It's not important."

"It's not important that you murdered six people?"

"No," the voice said. "And it's actually seven."

"Uh huh." Monochrome looked down and picked a bit of grime out from under a fingernail.

"Gaze upon the horror," the voice said.

"Okay, I'm going to give you a pass because you're clearly new at this, but that line—"

A spotlight flicked on and illuminated a non-superhero corpse in the middle of the room.

Monochrome walked toward it and looked down, cringing a little at the result of two dozen stab wounds. A thirty-something man, tan beneath all the gore, stared up at him with dead eyes. He squinted at the body.

"Am I supposed to know who that is?"

"Maybe the blood is clouding your vision. That's your best friend," the voice said.

"I don't think so," Monochrome said.

"Yes, it is."

Monochrome threw out his hands and looked toward the ceiling again. "Little help here?"

"Ricky Gomez," the voice said.

"Ricky Gomez? How is he my best friend? I haven't seen him since I was eleven."

"I know," the voice said. "Not since 1994."

Monochrome's face turned a lighter shade of grey. "I'm going to melt you so hard."

There was a short, pinching sensation at the back of his neck.

"No you're not," the voice whispered.

Monochrome turned to spot the source of the voice and the needle, but his vision had gone fuzzy. He swayed back and forth for a moment before collapsing in a heap.

Monochrome awoke nauseated and hanging from a pipe by a pair of furry pink handcuffs from a novelty shop. Another becaped man hung nearby, his own pipe bent under his weight. The Immortal Man, America's favorite superhero, greeted his new neighbor.

"Why would you come alone?" the Immortal Man asked.

Monochrome blinked as his eyes adjusted to flickering fluorescent light. "Why wouldn't I?"

"Because you're more likely to be kidnapped alone?"

Monochrome ignored him. "What was Defense Squad Z even doing here?"

"We assumed you wouldn't show, so we came to rescue the hostages," the Immortal Man said.

"*Hostage*," Monochrome corrected.

"*Hostages*," the Immortal Man re-corrected. "We just didn't realize *we* were going to be the hostages."

With his vision focused, Monochrome eyed the man from head to toe and back to head. "You're covered in blood."

"Yeah, my murder didn't take."

Monochrome nodded. "Because you're immortal. Got it."

He glanced up at the pipe and handcuffs and thought about melting things. Nothing melted, and he squinted in annoyance.

"You don't seem impressed," the Immortal Man said.

"What's there to be impressed by?" Monochrome asked.

That was a reasonable question considering the man next to him looked like the prototypical comic relief. He was chubby for a superhero, and his hair was not a beautiful, romance cover blond but the kind that might have been white hair with some mustard stains. It fell limply at the sides of his pasty face.

Monochrome continued. "I met an immortal once before. He died. Not impressive."

The Immortal Man formally introduced himself. "Well, I'm Hudson Marrow. Nice to meet—"

"I know who you are. And you know who I am. You stole my idea."

"*Excuse me?*"

"To make a superhero team."

"You're not the first person to come up with that idea," the Immortal Man said. "I promise. You can trace the concept back to Gilgamesh if you want to—"

Monochrome cut the know-it-all off. "I would have been the first person to do it IRL."

"Well, technically you pretended to be a superhero for years, so there was no reason to think you'd ever make good on your promise."

"Ugh. Shut up."

"Those are the words of someone who knows they have no point," the Immortal Man said.

"Yeah?" Monochrome asked. "Well, *those* are the words of a forty-year-old neckbeard."

"I'm actually fifty-two. I look younger because—"

"Oh my God, I get it. You're immortal. No one cares." Monochrome's voice took a cheerier tone as he changed subjects. "So what's going on here with evil voice guy—"

"Silence!" The disembodied voice returned, and Monochrome rolled his eyes at the air.

He jerked back when the face appeared in front of him. In person it was clearly scarred and attached to a disfigured body. One thing was instantly recognizable: the blue half-goatee that sprouted from a scabbed and peeling chin.

"Yikes," Monochrome said. "You're that guy."

"You recognize me then?" the man said.

"You recognize him?" the Immortal Man asked.

"You did this to me!" the man said.

"Not intentionally," Monochrome said.

"You *melted his face*?" the Immortal Man asked.

"Again, not intentionally. He was going to hit me with his truck!"

"So you melted it? Couldn't you have just stepped out of the way?" the Immortal Man asked.

"You weren't there," Monochrome said. "I didn't burn him. The fire in his truck did."

"I saw the video on the news. My entire team is dead because you couldn't think to *step to the side*?"

The goateed man began a despairing rant. "Life was good before you freaks..."

Monochrome rolled his eyes again. "Do I really have to listen to your bit? Just kill me."

The man's eyes narrowed. "You gave my daughter powers. You wanna guess what kind?"

Monochrome leaned his head back. "Something terrible, I'm sure."

"She grew a set of gills. We had to release her into the East River."

Monochrome tried to put some PR spin on that. "Well, she's alive—"

"She is not," the man said.

"I'm sorry to hear that?" Monochrome wasn't very good

at sounding sorry.

"My wife's not either. She was eaten on Coney Island."

"By the sea monster we stopped?" Monochrome asked.

The man nodded. "Right before you killed my daughter."

"We didn't kill anyone," Monochrome said.

The man screamed into Monochrome's face. "My daughter's corpse was visible in your selfie!"

Monochrome shrunk back. "Ohhh, your kid was the sea monster. Yikes."

"It's too late to apologize." The man stepped away and began pacing. "I've taken care of Defense Squad Z, and soon I'll take care of the Bedazzlers."

The Immortal Man objected. "My team didn't do anything to you."

"And they never will," the man said.

"I don't have a team anymore," Monochrome said. "Did you even watch *Sergei & Tina*?"

"They'll come," the trucker said.

"No, they won't. They hate me." Monochrome paused. "Why can't I melt my cuffs?"

The trucker smirked. "Ask 'the Immortal Man.'"

"Don't put air quotes around it. I can't die," the Immortal Man said.

"That's what the last one said," Monochrome said.

The Immortal Man shook his head and returned to the topic at hand. "It's a souped-up muscle relaxant, essentially. I've been looking into ways to help people with undesirable powers."

"Aren't you a physicist?" Monochrome asked.

"I dabble," the Immortal Man said.

"You can't just dabble in a totally different field," Monochrome said. "That's ridiculous."

"You're an actor and a CEO and a superhero," the Immortal Man said.

"That's different," Monochrome said.

The Immortal Man rolled his eyes. "Of course it is. Anyway, someone broke into my lab about a week ago and stole it. I'm guessing *this guy* jabbed you with it."

The trucker gave a slow, sarcastic clap.

"How did he know what to take?" Monochrome asked. "Did you just label your superpower suppressant?"

"Of course I did. That's basic lab safety."

"And why aren't you dead? He didn't prick you with it?"

"I'm not going to invent a formula that works against me. That's basic self-preservation."

"And is your formula why I feel like I'm going to puke?" Monochrome asked.

"Probably," the Immortal Man said.

"Ugh, you douchebags. Just kill me," Monochrome said.

The trucker let out a dramatic cackle. "Not until the Bedazzlers are here to watch."

"There. Are. No. Bedazzlers."

"They'll come," the trucker said, dramatically pulling out his phone.

18

SOLO ADVENTURES II : MAGMA BOOGALOO

Doctor Queer was not a drinker. He believed it distracted him from his purpose and damaged his ability to focus on divine dimensionmastering. Like most carbon-based life forms, however, he was an eater; so Percival turned his drink invitation into a lunch invitation. The nemeses met at O'Gilligan's, a chain restaurant specializing in "good food, good friends, and good memories."

"Why Times Square?" Doctor Queer asked.

Percival spoke with a touristy glow. "Well, it's not every day I'm in *New York City*."

"You're one hundred and thirty years old," Doctor Queer said. "Surely you've toured New York."

"I visited Staten Island once at the turn of the century. I didn't see anything worth returning for."

"No, I don't suppose you would have."

Doctor Queer glanced at the decor with contempt. Having lived through two centuries' worth of architectural trends, he could appreciate a number of styles. He could not, however, appreciate cartoon bears made of bottlecaps and wooden signs adorned with misspelled folksy sayings. One especially annoying sign ("I keep trying to loose weight but it keeps finding me") bored into his brain, damaging his focus.

Also distracting was the meal that had just been delivered

to the man sitting across from him. The dread Percival was a vegan, and Doctor Queer eyed his tofu wrap with suspicion.

"You have attempted to end the world on dozens of occasions," Doctor Queer noted.

"That's unfair," Percival said. "I've attempted to end *humanity* on several occasions."

"Still. I find it strange your disregard for human life doesn't extend to all life."

"*People* are the problem," Percival said.

"I don't disagree," Doctor Queer said. "I disagree with your solution."

"Come now. Your family is dead. You tried working with that team of costumed ruffians, and that was a disaster. What would be so wrong with people not existing?"

Doctor Queer answered dryly. "Well, you wouldn't have O'Gilligan's, for starters."

"I wouldn't have a human-run O'Gilligan's," Percival said. "I'm open to robots, simulations, or alternative dominant lifeforms."

"That's not your decision to make. Besides, sometimes human beings are... surprising... in what they're capable of."

"I'm not buying it," Percival said.

"Yes you are. You invited me here."

Percival smirked. "You telling a joke is more surprising than anything I've ever seen a human being do."

"I am human," Doctor Queer said. "Loosely."

"Very loosely. And I *do* hate you, don't forget."

For the third time in twenty minutes, Doctor Queer's phone rang.

Percival shook his head. "Someone *desperately* wants to get ahold of you."

Doctor Queer answered it this time and was confronted by Blanche's off-putting accent. He would have ignored her call, but he'd forgotten to save her number.

"We can't get to the freakin' Bedazzlestation," she said. "Our badges have been canceled."

"Who is 'we'? There are no Bedazzlers."

"Me and Jack. We've got a doozy of a situation."

"What's that?" Doctor Queer said.

"Human beings surprising you?" Percival asked.

Doctor Queer put up a finger to silence him as Blanche explained what she'd seen on *Sergei & Tina*.

"Come to my home," Doctor Queer said into the phone. "We'll convene and determine a course of action from there."

Percival repeated himself with a smirk. "Human beings surprising you?"

"Yes, actually..."

On the other end of the surprise spectrum, Brooks and Smith were arguing.

Don't answer it, Smith said.

I've not answered it <u>six times</u>, Brooks said.

Well, don't answer it seven times, Smith said.

Their Afterlife™ scenario du jour was Titanic Before It Sank, and because the people who researched and programmed The Afterlife™ were lazy, it was based almost entirely on the movie *Titanic* rather than the actual ship. In the real world, Brooks's cell phone was ringing. In the fake world, the two had crammed into the back of a 1912 Renault.

Smith halted his belt removal to complain. *Every time.*

Smith wanted to re-enact the car scene. It was, in his words, "the only good thing about that fucking movie." Patience and Lemon had gone trash hunting at the park, so Brooks's body sat alone. Every bit of the pair's focus could be dedicated to this scenario, in theory.

I had a sexual awakening to Titanic, Smith said.

You were already twenty-something when it came out, Brooks said. *You'd already had sex with several people.*

Smith stared at him. *Several is a light estimate, but so what?*

So I don't think you know what a sexual awakening is, Brooks said. *And besides, I can both answer the phone out there and have sex with you in here. It's called multitasking—*

—And you're terrible at it, Smith noted.

It really doesn't take that much focus to get plowed in the back of a Renault, Brooks said.

This is serious fetish shit. You can't half-ass it.

Then you're going to have to wait, Brooks said. *I'm taking the call.*

Abby had finally figured out the wolf-man's transformation scene, but was stuck on the part where the creature was to make love to Catalina. There were only so many euphemisms for sex, and she'd used nearly all of them in her first novel, *The Bat-King and I.* She sat in the bullpen at the *New York Tribune,* which housed all five people on staff. The newspaper had mistakenly hitched its wagon to print. It was the only paper in New York that boasted no online edition and was distributed exclusively via adolescent paperboys, either on fixed-gear bicycles or on foot. The Tribune made more money from "Read Local" bumper stickers and tote bags than it did from newspapers.

A woman's voice confronted Abby from across the room. "Waters!"

As the kitten on her "Hang in There" poster judged her work ethic, Abby quickly minimized the wolf story and maximized an in-progress article on pumpkin carving.

Rita Jenkins, senior editor and source of the voice, confronted her. "What are you doing here?"

"Working?" Abby said.

"You wanted to cover Monochrome," Rita said. "Go cover him."

"I have everything I need for the Bedazzlers article."

"Is that so?" Rita asked.

Abby nodded, smug. No one in New York had more on the Bedazzlers than she did.

"Do you have a write-up for how this Coney Island situation is going to play out?" Rita asked.

"The what?" Abby asked.

"Oh, for crying out— *Watch the news!*"

Abby pointed out an inconvenient fact. "We can't. They cut our cable because the *Tribune* stopped paying the bill."

"There's news on the internet," Rita said.

"We had *cable internet*," Abby said.

"You people have cell phones," Rita said.

"You make us lock them in a cabinet before we enter the newsroom," Abby said. "What was it you said? We'd 'get distracted by Hokeyblock Blast and never get anything done'?"

Rita groaned. "Whatever. Check now. Go to Coney Island. You're on the case."

Abby retrieved her phone from the cabinet and found that she'd missed fourteen calls from an unknown number. She grabbed her things as she listened to her voicemail and then rushed out the door.

Jack and Blanche didn't expect the woman who welcomed them into the Nakamura home. They knew that Ana often worried about disappointing her family, so they expected a pair of uptight, high-expectations parents. The cheery woman who hugged both of them and lovingly directed them to her living room didn't seem to fit the bill.

"Come in. Come in," she said. "Have a seat."

As Blanche lowered herself onto a taupe recliner, Mrs. Nakamura rushed over and gently stopped her from sitting.

"That seat's for the Head of the Household."

Blanche scratched her head. "Oh. Um. Sorry?"

As Blanche moved to the couch where Jack sat, Mrs. Nakamura moved toward the kitchen. "Can I offer you a juice or some milk?"

Jack was put off. "No... thanks."

"I'll take the milk," Blanche said.

Jack gave her a look.

"What? It's freakin' rude to not take *something*."

When Mrs. Nakamura was out of earshot, Jack leaned in. "These people are weird."

"Right?" Blanche gestured around the room. "No TV. Chair rules."

"Wholesome board games everywhere," Jack added, gesturing at a shelf.

Before he could move on to critiquing the Precious Moments figurines, Mrs. Nakamura re-entered the room, glass of whole milk in hand.

"Sorry to just drop by," Blanche said. "We tried calling first."

Mrs. Nakamura handed Blanche the glass. "Oh, that's all right. There's no way you could have known that Ana's grounded from using her phone. I guess I could have answered it, but that's going a bit too far, don't you think?"

"Dunno," Blanche said. She turned away from everyone, lifted her balaclava slightly, and took a sip. She replaced it and moved to set her glass on the coffee table.

"Don't forget your coaster," Mrs. Nakamura said.

The coasters were patterned to look like quilts. Blanche admired one and then set her glass down in silence.

"Can we talk to her for a minute alone?" Jack asked.

Mrs. Nakamura pondered. "I really shouldn't let her, but

what the heck. Maybe you two can spread the word so people will know she's not allowed out."

Mrs. Nakamura stepped down the hallway to the office to retrieve Ana, who was busy holding hands with her father and licking envelopes to help with his business. When Mrs. Nakamura returned, she handed her daughter to Jack.

"Will ten minutes do the trick?" Mrs. Nakamura asked.

"That'll do. Thanks," Jack said.

They sat in silence until they were certain Ana's mother was gone.

"How can you be grounded?" Jack asked.

"Yeah, aren't you, like, twenty?" Blanche added.

"Twenty-one," Ana corrected. "House rules."

"Speaking of—" Jack started.

"We're Mormon," Ana said.

Jack was baffled. "How—"

"When I was twelve, my parents let a pair of missionaries in, thinking they were selling cookies. They didn't have the heart to kick them out, and now we're Mormon. They take the wholesomeness a bit too far."

"Huh," Jack and Blanche said at once.

"It's weird," Ana said, "but not any weirder than getting superpowers from magma dust."

Blanche put them back on topic. "So, what does the *Book of Mormon* say about breaking curfew and meeting up at Doctor Queer's place?"

"It doesn't have anything to say about that, but I'm sure my parents would," Ana noted.

"We can frame it as taking you *off their hands* for a little bit," Jack said.

Blanche shook her head. The joke was too lame, even for her, and Jack really was lucky she existed to be the group's punching bag.

"You guys don't need me," Ana said.

"Not true," Jack said. "The *Saw* ripoff guy was specific

about wanting the Bedazzlers. Whether you like it or not, you're a Bedazzler."

"What do you say?" Blanche asked.

Ana glanced around the room. This was an opportunity to break the rules for a good cause. The coast was clear, and she could ask forgiveness later. She smirked, and spoke at her usual drone. "Let's go bedazzling."

The phrase came out more sarcastic than rallying, but when she stood, it became apparent that she meant it, and they headed out.

19

SCHEMING

E verybody who was anybody had their eyes glued to the news. The same was true for everybody who was nobody, like the failures on the Reticent board. Their traffic jam robbery foiled by the Bedazzlers and their wine scheme foiled by Defense Squad Z, they hadn't much to be cheery about. That was, until they learned that one meddling superhero team had been destroyed and the other was soon to follow.

The headline at the bottom of the screen read "CONEY ISLAND SLAUGHTER, IS THE PRESIDENT TO BLAME?" and blonde-haired, blue-eyed pundits yelled over each other.

"Who is going to answer for the murder of Defense Squad Z?" the male pundit asked.

"You've seen the video," the female pundit said. "Clearly the bearded guy who murdered them is to blame."

"Yeah, but who sent Defense Squad Z in there? They worked for the President."

"They need presidential authorization. That doesn't mean it was the President's idea to send them. They probably asked and got approval to investigate." The female pundit was being far too reasonable, and her microphone cut out.

The male pundit butted in. "Once again, if you're just tuning in, we're sad to report that six of the seven members of Defense Squad Z are dead. If you want to pay respects, you can do so on our Twitter feed using the hashtag #ForeverZ."

In the frosty tent headquarters of the Reticent, Heidi Werewith cackled.

"This is perfect," she said.

"How?" Sarah asked.

"One annoying group of heroes dead, and the other disbanded. When the Bedazzlers don't rescue Godwin Zane, he'll be killed too, and there won't be any more interference at City Hall."

"Interference," one of the Webers whispered. Another giggled.

Werewith glared and the Webers shut up to listen to her. "Without Godwin Zane screwing us over, we'll get our permits back, and this company will be summoning wealthy ghosts and robbing people through portals in no time."

Travis Marsh didn't see things that way. He didn't see things at all, as his zombified eyes had fallen out of their sockets. His last tooth fell to the table as he spoke, and he frowned. "I hate to brrrrrraaa—break it to you, but Baig says they're meeting at Doctor Queer's house right now."

"What? When was someone going to tell me this?"

"He just did," Sarah said.

"All right, people," Werewith said. "We have one goal right now: keep the Bedazzlers away from Coney Island. I'm going to call in all the favors I have, but I'm going to need your help."

20

BEDAZZLERS CONVENE!

Doctor Queer's Riverdale mansion, with its twelve-foot ceilings and burgundy, draped curtains, was a modestly more comfortable base than the Bedazzlestation. Abby was the last to arrive, and Ana wished she was holding *her* hand rather than Brooks's chilly cyborg one. They'd been convening around the fireplace for ten minutes, but neither the hand nor the fireplace was warm.

Abby threw her jacket over a golden throne in the foyer and warmed her arms. "It was seventy degrees out last week. It's forty now." She stepped in front of the fireplace to immediate disappointment. "What's this nonsense?"

"The soothing fires of Barganoth," Doctor Queer said. "They facilitate collaboration."

"Do you have any warming fires of *fire*?" Abby asked.

"Right? Where's the magma guy when you need him?" Blanche asked.

Abby shook her head and retrieved her coat. As she did so, her gaze caught the grand staircase and vast rooms in every direction. "How can you afford this place?"

"Rutherford Hayes owed me a favor," Doctor Queer said.

"How many presidents have owed you a favor?" Abby asked.

"Several." The doctor gestured toward a doorway. "Please. This way."

This way led to the mansion's dining room, the kind of

dining room most people only see in movies. A table that could easily seat thirty rested atop an ornate rug. The walls, covered in elaborate gold wallpaper and mahogany wainscoting, were accented by tapestries and oil paintings of old white people.

Blanche flopped onto a chair. "Finally. I've been standing for hours."

"You live here alone?" Jack asked.

"That is correct," Doctor Queer said.

The stuffy abode reminded Jack of Cedar Acres. "That's kind of sad."

There were scattered nods.

"This home is located on the portal to R'kagn'stek," Doctor Queer said. "It is imperative that I have access to this in order to protect the world from—" He ran a finger through the dust on the table. "Yes. It is a bit sad."

"You should get an assistant," Jack said.

"I had one once," Doctor Queer said. "It didn't end well."

Ana found herself drawn to a shimmering, opal-bordered floor mirror. She dragged Brooks toward it. "What's this?"

Doctor Queer jumped between her and the mirror. "That's the Mirror of Regret."

She tried to peek around him. "So?"

"Gazing into it can leave the unprepared mind destroyed by guilt," Doctor Queer said.

"But what does it do?" Ana asked.

"It's the *Mirror of Regret*," Brooks said. "*I assume* it shows people stuff they regret."

"Yeah, and then they *regret* looking at it," Jack said.

No one laughed at Jack's joke.

Brooks gave Doctor Queer a gentle push out of the way and looked into the mirror. "Ah, yep. There's Eddie bleeding to death. Cool mirror."

He turned away from it and pretended he wasn't shaken. Ana patted his shoulder with her free hand.

Doctor Queer directed his attention to a different corner of the room, where Jack was running his fingers down the side of a bronze vase etched with dogs. "Stop touching ancient artifacts!"

"Why?" Jack asked. "What does this do?"

"That vase contains the soul of a Cerberus!" Doctor Queer warned.

"What about this?" Abby asked. She held up a smaller, golden container.

"Steve Irwin's ashes," Doctor Queer said.

"Wh—"

Doctor Queer grabbed a utensil from Blanche's hand. "Don't touch the Fork of Contempt."

Blanche crossed her arms and propped her feet up on the table. "We shoulda been headquartered here all along instead of the spooky skeleton lair."

Ana nodded. "This is way better."

Brooks shrugged his free arm. "Well, it's irrelevant now since we're not a team."

"That's why we're here," Abby said.

Brooks groaned.

"Have you watched the news lately?" Jack asked.

"No. Why would I do that?" Brooks asked.

"Because it's even worse than *Sergei & Tina*," Jack said.

Doctor Queer shouted "*projectens*" and various news stations began playing in mid-air at the center of the table. He went blind and could only hear the reports.

The others saw everything. Cell phone footage prepared by a murderous trucker zoomed in on the corpses of Defense Squad Z, one by one. Anchors spoke over each other with phrases like "shocking footage" and "viewer discretion" as the screen filled with lightly blurred blood and gore.

"It's unclear what abilities this man has," one anchor said. "What is clear is that he's powerful, dangerous, and has hostages."

The camera pointed at Monochrome and the Immortal Man, hanging unconscious from their pipes. Dramatic bass punctuated even more dramatic words. "If the rest of the Bedazzlers aren't here by midnight tonight, these two will be the first to die, but they won't be the last. I keep time very closely. When I say midnight, I mean midnight. If they show up at 12:01, these guys will already be dead."

"Kinda hokey, ain't he?" Blanche asked.

"Indeed," Doctor Queer said, without a hint of self-awareness.

Abby shrugged. "Yeah, but—"

Brooks groaned in expectation of where this conversation was going.

"We need to get him out of there," Abby said.

Ana nodded.

"Why?" Brooks asked.

"*Why?*" Abby mimicked.

"Yes. Why. He wouldn't walk into a murder lair for any of us," Brooks said.

"That's probably true," Jack said.

"So I'm just saying... maybe we let him die?"

Everyone looked at him, stunned.

"When they made you a cyborg, did they make you evil too?" Abby asked.

That's what I've been saying, Smith said.

You have literally never said that, Brooks said.

Well, I agree with her, Smith said.

"I don't know what they did," Brooks said. "They didn't give me a manual. You think it's evil to not care whether *Monochrome* dies?"

"Kinda," Blanche said.

"Pretty much," Ana said.

"Yeah, dude," Jack said.

Brooks sighed. "What's the point of putting our lives in danger to save people who aren't worth saving?"

"Well in *your* case, the point is to get that robot body," Jack said.

"Yeah, that's never going to happen," Brooks said.

"You don't know that," Abby said. "Plus he's not the only one who needs to be saved."

"The Immortal Man is *immortal*," Brooks noted.

So was I, Smith said.

You aren't helping.

Doctor Queer folded his arms and turned his face toward what he believed was Brooks's general direction. "I told you not to stare into the Mirror of Regret."

"The point is to help people," Ana said. "It's not supposed to be conditional, or we'd find some reason everyone isn't worth saving."

"I've been helping people for *over a decade*. This is what I have to show for it." Brooks gestured at his bandaged arm. "A cyborg body with evil programming, a dead husband living in my head, and PTSD."

"Oh shit," Abby said, with realization. She reached a hand toward Ana. "Come here."

Ana let go of Brooks's hand.

"Feel any better?" Abby asked.

"Not really," Brooks said. "You want a vote on whether we go after him. I vote no."

Abby glared at him. "I vote yes."

"Me too," Blanche said. "He seemed really sincere on *Sergei & Tina*."

Jack faked a cough. "I wouldn't know about that, but he did go after the guy on Coney Island. Maybe he wouldn't walk into *this* trap to save us, but he didn't have to go in the first place."

"He probably only did it for the PR," Brooks said.

"That may well be true," Doctor Queer said.

"That's absolutely true," Brooks said.

"Still," Abby said.

"Still," Jack said.

Ana nodded. "Still."

"We were called out," Jack said. "If we don't do anything, we're responsible for whatever happens."

"No, the evil guy who wishes he was in a horror movie is responsible for whatever happens," Brooks said.

The other Bedazzlers shrugged.

Babe— Smith started.

"*Fine*," Brooks said. He was actually starting to feel better.

Blanche, tendering her best Monochrome impression, jumped up from her seat and raised a fist to the air. "To Coney Island!"

"Um…" Ana stared at her. "…Maybe we should wait until Arch can see?"

Jack agreed. "Yeah, and until he can summon our costumes for us."

"Cripes," Blanche said. "I really wanted to do the thing."

The rest of the group shook their heads.

21
LOCATION, LOCATION, LOCATION

The following are ideas Monochrome had while hanging from a pipe for over an hour: ceiling fans shaped like UFOs, self-leveling picture frames, mind-reading grocery drones, officially licensed Bedazzlers action figures, cloud-based repressed memory storage, shoes that are also drones, collars for cats to communicate with birds, pep talk chapstick, greying mirrors for non-grey humans, chastepolines for people uncomfortable with the word *tramp*, and bees that make vinegar instead of honey.

He eyed his pocket. "I need to use my phone."

"Why?" the trucker asked.

"So I can send the team this address on the off chance they decide to come here."

"I gave them an address," the trucker said.

"No you didn't," Monochrome said. "You were weirdly specific about the time, *again*, but no address."

"As much as I hate to agree with Monochrome, I don't think you gave an address," the Immortal Man said.

The trucker took a seat. "Fuck. I'm such an idiot."

"First time holding people hostage and murdering them?" Monochrome asked.

"Yeah. Go ahead and call them." The trucker talked himself back into villain mode and shook a fist. "I need them here so they can *die*."

"Hey, Hot Stuff," Monochrome said.

The phone at his side let out a jingle, and Hot Stuff replied. "What do you need?"

"Send group message to Bedazzlers: 2994 ½ Cropsey Avenue. Soon would be good."

"Message sent, you magnificent bastard," Hot Stuff said.

The Immortal Man blinked in disbelief. His Zanephone never called him a magnificent bastard. It called him "virgin" and "science nerd."

Monochrome rolled his neck to stretch, then looked from the Immortal Man to their kidnapper and back. "This is boring," he said.

"Should I be sorry for that?" the trucker asked. "You're hostages."

"I mean, it's kind of like you're not entertaining your house guests," Monochrome said.

"What does it matter? I'm going to kill you."

Monochrome stretched again. "Come on. If I'm bored, you're bored. Work with me here."

"I'm not bored," the trucker said, deepening his voice. "I'm eagerly anticipating *your death*."

"Yuh huh," Monochrome said.

"Incoming message," Hot Stuff said. "Torpedo: Have you tried escaping?"

Monochrome thought melting thoughts. Still nothing. "Hot Stuff, send group message to Bedazzlers: Yes I've tried escaping. Do you think I'm an idiot?"

The reply chime was almost instant.

"Incoming message," Hot Stuff said. "Agent Brooks: Yes."

"Okay," Monochrome said. "That was way too quick. Note to self: we might be able to use cyborg reaction times for—"

"Incoming message. Cactus Jack: Yes."

"Incoming message. Torpedo: Yes."

"Incoming message. Human Touch: Yes."

"Incoming message. Blanche: Yes."

No more messages arrived, and Monochrome sighed in relief. "At least Arch—"

"Incoming message," Hot Stuff said. "Doctor Queer: Thumbs up emoji, thumbs up emoji, thumbs up emoji, checkmark, okay hand gesture, checkmark, checkmark, aubergine emoji."

The Immortal Man shifted on his pipe and turned to face Monochrome. "They really don't like you, do they?"

"What?" Monochrome asked. "We have a great rapport. Playful banter is what it is—"

"Incoming message," Hot Stuff said. "Agent Brooks: If I don't get a robot body for Eddie after this, I'm going to stab you in the eye."

Monochrome faked a laugh. "He's joking. Like I said, great rapport."

"Incoming message. Agent Brooks: I'm serious."

If looks could cut, the scowl the Immortal Man gave Monochrome was one of R.J. Fillenputty's extra-large specialty chef's knives. "Maybe you should start thinking of a better escape plan than hoping your powers come back soon."

"I'm right here," the trucker said. "There's not going to be an escape."

"Incoming message," Hot Stuff said. "Torpedo—"

"No. That's enough." The trucker grabbed the Zanephone from Monochrome's side, dropped it onto the floor, and stomped it a dozen times with his boot.

"Hey!" Monochrome said. "She might have been agreeing to go on a date with me."

"I somehow doubt that," the Immortal Man said.

"I don't care," the trucker said. "The only appointment that matters is her appointment with *her doom*."

Monochrome rolled his eyes. "Ugh. Guy—"

"I have a name," the trucker said.

"What is it?" the Immortal Man asked.

"I'm not telling either of you."

"Guy it is, then," Monochrome said. "Guy. We're all bored here. Let's do something to pass the time. Anything."

"No. The Bedazzlers could arrive any moment. I have to be ready to fight—"

"The team disbanded, you idiot. But if they do show up, it'll be right up against the deadline."

"How do you figure?"

Monochrome spoke smugly. "If these were ambitious people, the team would be named after *their* favorite movies, not mine."

The Immortal Man squinted. "Your favorite movie is *Bedazzled*?"

"Yes. Obviously," Monochrome said.

"The original or the remake?"

"Ugh. If I could magma, I would melt you for that."

"*SHUT UP!*" the trucker said. "Both of you just shut up."

"Or what?" Monochrome asked. "You'll kill me? I'm already dead from boredom."

"And I can't die, so—"

Monochrome rattled the pipe. "Oh my God. We *get it!* You're immortal. Congratulations!"

The trucker covered his ears. "*SHUT UP. SHUT UP. SHUT UP.*"

Monochrome turned to the Immortal Man. "Hey, how long does it take to get through one round of '99 bottles'?"

"I don't know." The Immortal Man ran through a verse in his mind. "Probably like twelve seconds."

Monochrome did some mental math. "Five verses a minute, sixty minutes an hour, eleven hours to midnight..." He started singing. "*Three thousand bottles of beer on the wall, three thousand bottles of beer. Take one down, pass it around, two thousand nine hundred and ninety-nine bottles of beer on the wall...*"

22

THE LONG ROAD

I n most works of fantasy, there's at least one chapter in which the characters do nothing but walk toward their destination. This is that chapter.

"I'm perfectly willing to teleport us," Doctor Queer said.

They'd been over this a few times, but the team wouldn't go along with it.

"It's not a good idea," Torpedo said. "The guy who has Monochrome—whoever he is—managed to take down all of Defense Squad Z. You'd be frozen in place, helpless."

"We're already frozen in place," Brooks said.

To his (and everyone else's) chagrin, they had to move through Times Square to reach their destination. Arms bumped into arms, legs bumped into legs, arms bumped into legs, legs bumped into the sides of buildings, and so on. It was never clear whether the visible puffs of hazy air coming from tourists' mouths were from warm breath meeting the cold or from fourteen-dollar packs of menthols.

By subway, the Bedazzlers had made it as far as 42nd Street before a mysterious track closure transformed them into pedestrians. They sought the next entrance that would put them on the Q train toward Coney Island, but walking was a huge pain, especially for one member of the team.

"I wish this costume didn't have heels," Human Touch complained. "It's fine for standing around holding hands, but for *this*?"

Torpedo opened her faceplate. "I'm with you. This armor is starting to feel heavy."

Blanche patted her puffy coat. "I'm tellin' ya. This is why I dress for comfort."

"You dress like that because you're a danger to everyone," Brooks noted.

"Well, yeah, but I do it for the comfort too."

Cactus Jack poked at her coat. "We've walked almost a mile. You have to be sweltering under there."

Blanche shrugged.

Human Touch tugged at Cactus Jack's arm and nudged her head toward a shop window. "Party store."

"You want to get another mask?" he asked.

"No. They'll have flip-flops," Human Touch said. "But also, I kind of want another mask."

"People have already seen the selfie," Torpedo said.

"It *is* plausible deniability, though," Cactus Jack said.

"Exactly," Human Touch said.

"We *do* have plenty of time," Torpedo said. "I guess—"

Before she could finish that thought, Human Touch and Cactus Jack bounded into the party store. The other Bedazzlers followed and soon found themselves entranced by aisles upon aisles of inexpensive and unnecessary favors. Doctor Queer gazed at starter magic kits as Torpedo eyed werewolf costumes. Brooks stood bewildered by the size of the store's plastic hat selection while Blanche circled the store on a quest to find a Halloween costume for Butternut.

Cactus Jack and Human Touch found the flip-flops with ease. Selecting a pair was not as easy.

"Sparkles or sequins?" Human Touch asked, not expecting an answer. "Red or white?"

Cactus Jack just stared at her.

Human Touch sighed. "I wish Teresa were here. She'd love this."

"It's just a party store," Cactus Jack said.

Brooks turned from the hats to the flip-flops. *I can't take it anymore. I have to know.*

Ugh. Here we go, Smith said.

What? Brooks asked.

Nothing, noseypants. I'm very interested in hearing her backstory. Smith, not at all interested, popped back into *Firefly* Season Two and tried to tune out reality.

Brooks walked over and took Human Touch's hand. "Hey, Jack, Blanche is looking for you where New Year's meets Earth Day."

When Cactus Jack was out of earshot, Brooks spoke softly. "Your assistant was your girlfriend."

"Please don't—"

"I'm not going to out you. Christ."

"How did you know?" Human Touch asked.

"How would I know? Really?" Brooks raised an eyebrow. "I just wanted to say that, whenever you decide to tell your family—if you do—it won't be as bad as you think."

Smith heard that and groused. *Could be.*

"They will kill me," Human Touch said.

"Statistically speaking, they probably won't," Brooks said.

"You're not very comforting," Human Touch said.

"I'm just saying... it will probably be fine. And if it's not fine, it will still be worth it."

Yeah, it was a real treat for me, Smith said.

Don't you have some piloting to do or something?

That's Wash's job. I'm just saying... not everyone is you.

Brooks took that to heart and corrected his generalization. "...*For me*, the weight off my shoulders was worth it. Lying sucks, and I felt like keeping this secret was actually crushing me, like I could feel pressure in my chest. And my dad didn't like it at first, but it didn't matter. As soon as I told him, that pressure was gone."

Human Touch stared at him, unsure whether the cyborg was done rambling.

"If you ever want to talk, I'm here," Brooks said.

"Thanks." She held up a pair of flip-flops. "Sparkles or sequins?"

Brooks squinted. "How would I know?"

Meanwhile, where the New Year's section met the Earth Day section, Cactus Jack ran up to Blanche.

"Brooks said you wanted to see me," he said.

"Hmm?" Blanche wondered. "Well, I guess so."

"What are you doing?" Cactus Jack asked.

"Checkin' out the Earth Day knitting patterns. I think I could tweak that Earth hat pattern and turn it into a costume for Butternut."

"You want to dress your cat as the planet?" Jack asked.

"Uh, yeah."

Cactus Jack's eyes went wide. "That... is... the most adorable thing I've ever pictured."

"Right!?"

Blanche held the pattern up with one hand and squinted at it, pondering.

"I never thanked you earlier," Cactus Jack said, "for not telling everyone I watch *Sergei & Tina*."

Blanche made a *pashaw* sound and waved his concern away. "You need me to be the lame one, I'm good for it. I ain't tryin' to impress anybody."

"What *are* you trying to do? I never really got that."

"Just tryin' to do right by myself and Butternut, is all. Who are you tryin' to impress?" she asked.

"You know, I don't know. When I was younger, my family moved around a lot. I guess I got used to being desperate to fit in," Cactus Jack said.

He reached for the shelf and grabbed a cactus chain party banner, then flipped it over and read the description out loud. "Earth isn't just a place for trees. It's a place for cactuses. Celebrate our planet with this party banner, perfect for your Earth Day shindig or a cowboy-themed birthday party."

"Do folks really have Earth Day parties?" Blanche wondered.

Cactus Jack gave the package a little shake. "I kind of want this so I can hang it in the Bedazzlestation."

"Get it," Blanche said.

"Nah, it's dumb and I will *never* hear the end of it."

Blanche leaned in close so Jack could see her staring through the goggles. "Just get it."

In another corner of the store, Torpedo decided that none of the werewolf costumes resembled what she had in mind and made her way to where Doctor Queer stood emitting a soft white glow.

"What are you doing?" she asked.

Doctor Queer put his crossed fingers to his temples. "I am imbuing a few of these kits with real magic."

"That sounds dangerous," Torpedo said.

"Hardly. Some children will wave their wands and a few sparks will shoot out."

"What's the cost of that?"

"It will reduce my lifespan, slightly."

Torpedo tilted her head. "How much is slightly?"

"A few months, give or take. I consider it worthwhile to spark some interest in the arcane. I'll require a replacement some day, you know."

"You don't seem to mind talking about your inevitable death..."

"No," Doctor Queer said. "I'll almost certainly die in battle defending this dimension, as it should be."

Torpedo had an idea. "How do you think I'm going to die?"

"It's crude to speculate," Doctor Queer said.

"Come on. I love speculating. It's my job to speculate."

Doctor Queer put a hand to his chin and pretended to think. "A sexual release of magma?"

She smacked his shoulder. "*Come on.* Let's get out of here."

Back outside, Cactus Jack and Blanche tucked their party favors into their jacket and coat pockets.

Human Touch ripped the tag off her brand-new mask—a full-face yellow number with a giant black hashtag on the forehead—and placed it on her face. It completely clashed with her brand-new, blue sequined flip-flops. Monochrome would hate it, and that was perfect.

Doctor Queer, meanwhile, put his hand to the side of his face in an attempt to cover it. "Everyone act casual. Don't look across the—"

"Why? What's across the street?" Torpedo asked.

A voice carried from across the street. "Archibald!"

Doctor Queer dropped his hand and slouched. "Percival."

The dread Percival sauntered across the street to reunite with his nemesis. "I thought you were one of the costumed characters for a moment. Look at this."

Percival unlocked his cell phone and swiped to show a selfie of himself with Elmo. He beamed. "Can you believe this place?" He swiped to show another photo, in which he stood next to Spider-Man. "It's amazing!"

The Bedazzlers stood curbside in a line, staring.

Blanche spoke first. "Who the heck—"

Doctor Queer sighed and introduced everyone. "Bedazzlers, this is the dread Percival, my sworn nemesis. Percival, the Bedazzlers. That's Cactus Jack, Blanche, Agent Brooks, Human Touch, and Torpedo."

"The pleasure is all mine," Percival said.

"It really is," Brooks said.

Percival squinted and approached Brooks. "You look familiar."

"I was a CEO. You must have seen me on *Entrepreneurity Hour* or something," Brooks said.

"No," Percival said. "That's not it."

"You know this guy?" Cactus Jack asked.

Torpedo eyed Percival's leather speedo. "I want to hear

that story."

"I don't know him," Brooks insisted.

Percival squinted again, and his eyes glowed red as he recalled an accurate history. "Yes you do. We met on Staten Island at the turn of the century. You've aged, and your right eye appears to be a different color."

Doctor Queer folded his arms. "So when you told me you visited New York at the turn of the century, you meant the year 2000?"

"You think I would have visited in 1900? Consider the pollution, Archibald."

"Oh no," Brooks said.

Oh yes, Smith said.

"You *are* from Staten Island," Blanche noted.

Torpedo snickered. "Did you sleep with Percival?"

"No. I didn't," Brooks said. "There's no way."

"My memory is eternal," Percival said. With orange, glowing hands, he traced the shape of a square into the air. It was a window to another time, and on the other side of time, a much younger Brooks approached Percival.

Brooks cringed. "I don't think anyone's interested in this."

"Are you kidding?" Cactus Jack asked.

"We *so* are," Torpedo said.

I definitely am, Smith said. He transferred himself to the Movie Theater scenario so he could grab some popcorn. As he kicked his feet up on the rail in front of his seat, the screen began mirroring the real world.

Brooks buried his head in his hands as his teammates watched him embarrass himself. His mind filled with his husband's cackling as the young Brooks flirted with Percival.

"I haven't seen you around here," the young Brooks said.

"Kill me," present-day Brooks said.

"And miss your reaction to this?" Torpedo scoffed.

Brooks pleaded. "I thought it was a costume. *I was nineteen.*"

"He was over a hundred," Doctor Queer said.

Smith struggled to speak between laughs. *You were thirsty for the dread Percival.*

You still slept with Monochrome, Brooks snipped.

Yeah, because I wanted to get magma blasted to death. Smith laughed. *You were hot for a purple centenarian.*

"Shall we gaze into an hour later?" Percival asked.

Brooks stepped in front of the magic window and waved his hands. "I think everyone gets it, thanks. I slept with a demon from another dimension."

Percival's voice lowered alongside his eyebrows. "'Demon' is a slur."

"I'm not sorry," Brooks said.

Torpedo wanted to make sure she got all of this down. "Hot Stuff, have you been recording?"

"Of course," Hot Stuff said.

Cactus Jack spoke with giddiness. "You will never live this down."

"I know," Brooks said. "Thank you. I know."

You can never judge me again, Smith said.

Brooks could, and he did. *You have two dragon tattoos.*

Doctor Queer tried to get back to their mission. "Percival, what do you want?"

"Nothing," Percival said. "I saw you and thought I'd say 'hello.' Oh, and I don't want to destroy humanity anymore."

Doctor Queer blinked. "I beg your pardon?"

"This place is incredible," Percival said.

"No, it's not. It's awful," Brooks said.

Aww, a lovers' spat, Smith said.

"I'm going to live here amongst these colorful humans," Percival said. "They're noisy and they smell terrible. I love it here in the time square."

"Well, congratulations," Doctor Queer said. "I'm glad to see Elmo was able to convince you of what I've been unable to for decades."

"Thank you," Percival said. Then he stood perfectly still,

making everyone uncomfortable.

"What?" Doctor Queer asked.

Percival held out a hand. "Aren't you going to tip me for the window trick?"

"I don't carry cash," Doctor Queer said. "Do any of—?"

There were scattered headshakes.

"Oh for—" Brooks pulled out a five-dollar bill and handed it to Percival.

Smith snickered. *How much can you get for that?*

A few blocks and rounds of teasing Agent Brooks later, the team stepped away from yet another set of orange barriers. It seemed every subway station in Manhattan had been shut down for one reason or another.

"I can't go on like this," Human Touch said, pulling at one of her flip-flops. "These might be worse than the heels."

"They *were* 99 cents," Torpedo noted.

Brooks hoisted Human Touch over his shoulder. "Is that better?"

"Yes. Thanks." It was a lot better, but Human Touch couldn't leave it there. "Did you ever do this to Percival?"

The rest of the Bedazzlers laughed.

"We're corrupting her," Cactus Jack said.

"Totally," Torpedo said. She grinned at the notion that the intern was becoming more comfortable with her teammates.

There was a brief silence before Doctor Queer chimed in. "At least we haven't all been corrupted by Percival."

The group laughed again.

Brooks rolled his eyes. "We're still doing this?"

"Uh, yeah," Cactus Jack said.

"What else are we supposed to do during this freakin' walk?" Blanche asked.

"Hang on," Torpedo said. "Hey, Hot Stuff."

"What do you need?" Hot Stuff asked.

"What time is it?" Torpedo asked.

"Three o'clock in the afternoon," Hot Stuff said.

Torpedo crossed her arms. "Seriously, these transit delays aren't normal. The news doesn't have anything about them. It's like the problem is following us. We should go down there and see if anything weird is going on."

"We have nine hours to get to Coney Island," Blanche said. "We oughtta be okay."

"I don't want to cut it close, though," Torpedo said.

"We could just take a cab," Blanche suggested.

Cactus Jack nodded, but everyone else ignored her.

The entire team followed Torpedo down into the dimly lit station. There, at the edge of an empty platform, stood a freakishly tall ginger. Traffic Jam.

"We took you to jail," Torpedo said.

"Yeah," Traffic Jam said.

"How'd you get out?" Blanche asked.

"Like I'm going to tell you," Traffic Jam scoffed.

Cactus Jack motioned at the track. "Did you jam up the trains with red lights?"

Traffic Jam smirked. "Maybe."

From a distance came a sound that could have been a toilet flushing or a distant train. Brooks tilted his head at it and then looked back toward Traffic Jam. "Are you alone?"

"Maybe."

Brooks set Human Touch down and handed her to Jack. He dusted himself off and approached Traffic Jam.

"Beware," Doctor Queer said. "He can be... *frustrating*."

Traffic Jam's smile became smugger, somehow.

Brooks, already in a mood from the relentless mockery, strutted right up to him and punched him in the face. The cyborg punch was enough to send Traffic Jam falling backward onto the tracks.

"Dude!" Cactus Jack shouted.

Traffic Jam was out cold, and the red lights returned to green. As a booming horn sounded the approach of an incoming train, Torpedo swooped down onto the track and flew the villain to safety. She set him down and then walked over to Brooks and poked at his chest. "What do you think you're doing?"

"Solving the problem," Brooks said over the noise of the train. "The trains are working again, and now we have proof it was him."

"You can't attack someone until we know they're committing a crime," Cactus Jack said.

"Who's going to do anything about it?" Brooks asked.

The answer to that question was the NYPD officer who'd been watching over the station. He patted his hands dry and approached the group reaching for his cuffs.

"You've got to be kidding me," Brooks said.

"You are under arrest," the officer said. "You have the right to—"

Doctor Queer sighed and faced the officer. "*Quod dico.* You're going to abandon this station and leave us alone."

The officer tucked his handcuffs away and headed for the stairs. "Sorry about that."

"I know that one," Blanche said. "That's the mind control spell. Nobody tell Doctor Queer anything or—"

Traffic Jam, coming to, let out a dazed mumble. "Attack your teammates."

"Oh, crap," Blanche said.

"'Oh, crap' is right," Torpedo said. "Thanks, Blanche."

Doctor Queer assumed his spellcasting position. An unnerving blacklight glow emerged from his hands as he readied some dark magic.

"Don't attack your teammates," Cactus Jack said.

Doctor Queer lowered his hands. "Hmm?"

"Attack your teammates," Traffic Jam said.

"Don't attack your teammates."

"Attack your—"

Brooks knocked Traffic Jam out again with another punch.

Cactus Jack repeated himself, in case the last half-command counted. "Don't attack your teammates. Go hang out in the bathroom until your mind control wears off."

Doctor Queer obliged, leaving to spend the next thirty minutes in a graffiti-lined bathroom stall.

"I don't know if I like punching people unconscious," Torpedo said, "but—"

Blanche finished her thought. "But freakin' cripes. They don't come more annoying than that guy."

She was wrong. With a train now stopped at the station, its lone passenger emerged. Dressed in a beige unitard with a cartoon spring on the chest and brown gloves and boots was yet another powered human who fancied himself a rival for the Bedazzlers.

"You won't be going any farther today," the villain said as his train pulled away.

Torpedo groaned. "Who are you?"

"I am Arab Spring." He took a bow.

The Bedazzlers exchanged astonished glances.

"Man," Cactus Jack said. "We just want to get to Coney Island. We don't have a problem with you. We don't even know who you are."

"When I'm finished, you will," Arab Spring said, pulling at his fingers.

Human Touch gagged. "It's like he's made of silly putty."

"Hit him with some spikes," Brooks directed.

"What is *with* you?" Cactus Jack asked. "He hasn't even done anythin—"

Arab Spring stretched his fist across the station and knocked Blanche flat on her ass.

"Ow!" Blanche said. "What'd you do that for?"

"Because I can," Arab Spring said. He reached across again

and did the same to Torpedo.

Brooks turned to Cactus Jack. "You were saying?"

"Okay, maybe a few spikes to the leg."

Cactus Jack raised his arm and aimed.

He launched four spines toward the villain, but when they touched Arab Spring's skin, his stretchy body spread out of the way and the spines flew straight through him.

Human Touch gagged again, and Arab Spring somehow heard her over the sound of the next incoming train.

"It's not gross," Arab Spring said. He sprinted toward Human Touch, intending to tackle her.

Brooks pulled her out of the way, and the Arab Spring flew past where they were standing and bounced off a wall. Blanche, who was busy lifting herself off the ground, ducked to avoid being hit by the flying spring-man.

Torpedo stood and straightened herself. From under her faceplate came a mechanized gagging noise. In the distance, another train horn sounded.

Arab Spring landed and repeated himself. "It's not gross. *I'm* not gross."

"You're kinda gross," Blanche said.

At hearing Blanche, of all people, say that, Arab Spring bounded toward her. Blanche ducked, and the villain missed. He instead launched himself right in front of the next incoming train.

There was a THURNK noise, and chunks of silly putty flesh scattered throughout the station.

Human Touch put a fist to her mouth, suppressing another gag.

"Holy buckets," Blanche said.

"Well, that's..." Cactus Jack didn't have a word for it.

The train doors opened, and dozens of passengers filed out, ignoring the pieces of flesh at their feet and the smell of viscera in the air. They had places to be.

So did the Bedazzlers. Torpedo removed her faceplate,

wiped some sweat from her brow, and replaced it. She stepped forward. "That's our train."

"What about Arch?" Human Touch asked through her fist.

"That's *not* our train," Torpedo corrected.

It was time for more waiting.

23

WHAT WOULD MAGMA DO?

Monochrome tapped his fingers to a beat against the pipe to which he was chained. "*—two thousand eight hundred and thirty-four bottles of beer on the wall. Two thousand eight hundred and thirty-four bottles of beer. Take one down, pass it around, two thousand eight hundred and thirty-three bottles of beer on the—*"

One hundred and sixty-seven verses of "99 Bottles" is the tolerance limit for human beings, and the trucker snapped. He stormed over and wrapped his hands around Monochrome's throat.

The Immortal Man spoke in a calming tone. "You don't want to do this, guy."

The trucker tore his hands away from the billionaire's throat and threw them in the air. "Stop calling me 'guy'!"

Monochrome coughed a little. "Have you considered therapy, guy?"

"*STOP CALLING ME GUY!*"

"If you don't want to be 'guy,' tell us your name," Monochrome said.

"You can call me... the Trucker," the trucker said.

Monochrome laughed. "I will not. Seriously. What's your name?"

The villain sneered. "The Trucker."

"So you want to kill all the superheroes, but you also want to rip us off and take a codename?"

"My plans for myself are the same as they are for all of

you," the trucker said.

"Yikes," Monochrome said.

The Immortal Man tried to soothe him again. "Guy—"

The Trucker pulled a knife from his pocket and jabbed it into the Immortal Man's throat.

He let out a gargling sound. Blood sprayed in an arc, leaving a trail down Monochrome's left side as the Immortal Man fell unconscious.

"My *cape*," Monochrome complained.

As expected, the Immortal Man did what immortal men do. Skin stretched across the gash, stopping the blood flow and reviving him. "Trucker—"

"*The* Trucker," the trucker said.

"You don't address people with an article," Monochrome said.

The Immortal Man shushed him. "*The* Trucker, listen. Killing all the superheroes isn't going to bring your family back. It's not even going to kill all the heroes. You think more won't appear after the Bedazzlers are dead?"

"Then I'll kill them too," the trucker said.

"You're just a guy—"

"*STOP CALLING ME GUY.*"

"*A* guy," the Immortal Man said. "You'll be caught eventually and spend the rest of your life in jail. Is that what you want?"

Monochrome rolled his eyes. "I mean, he already killed people. He's going to jail either way."

The Immortal Man shushed him again. "Mr. Zane and I are willing to look the other way. If you let us go, we'll say the whole thing was a prank and you were an actor."

Monochrome choked back a laugh. "No we won't."

"Yes we will," the Immortal Man said.

"—Definitely not."

The Immortal Man snapped. "You're ruining my hostage negotiation."

"I'm not negotiating," the trucker said. "Did Ricky Gomez get to negotiate?"

"When *you killed him*?" Monochrome wondered. "Probably not."

"You know that's not what I meant. I'm talking about what the whole world's going to find out about *Monochrome*. I'm talking about when you—"

Monochrome sing-shouted over him. "—*LALLALALA ALA LALALALA. LALALA*—"

The Immortal Man eyed him. "I actually want to know what you did to—"

"*LALALALALALALA*—"

The trucker rifled through his things and pulled out a bottle of Xanax.

24

NOT THROWING AWAY THEIR SHOT

H aving bested a bevy of befuddling foes (and some transit delays), the Bedazzlers were finally ready to retrieve Monochrome. But as their feet hit the steps leading out of the Ocean Parkway station, Brooks's phone alert—a simple beep—went off.

"Oh my God," he said.

At the same time, Hot Stuff spoke to Torpedo. "Incoming Message. Read aloud?"

"No!" Torpedo said, pulling the phone from her armor.

Cactus Jack eyed both of them. "What?"

"I won the *Hamilton* lottery," Brooks said.

"I thought you didn't like it," Cactus Jack said.

"I don't, but I've entered it every day so Eddie can see it."

How the hell have you been doing that behind my back... er, behind my brain? Smith asked.

You know how I tell you to go away when I'm in the bathroom, and you tune out and putz around in the spaceship Enterprise?

Starship, Smith corrected.

Whatever. I've been entering it then, Brooks said. *Every day for a few months now.*

Holy shit. I love you.

"I won too," Torpedo said.

"No," Cactus Jack said. "That can't be possible. There are only like ten winners a night."

"Well, two of them are right here," Torpedo said, grinning.

She realized that no one could see her grin under her face-plate, so she took it off and then grinned again. "We won!"

"We can't be distracted by frivolities," Doctor Queer said. He implored Torpedo, as she seemed to have the most sense of the lot. "We have a mission. What was it you were just saying about not wanting to cut this close?"

Brooks tapped at his phone. "I just claimed my tickets."

"Me too," Torpedo said.

"We have a missio—"

"We have *Hamilton* tickets," Torpedo corrected. Reason was officially out the window, and she turned to Brooks. "Who are you gonna take?"

"Well, I planned on taking Lemon, but she's got a show in Cleveland tonight. So... you want to go, Jack?"

"Do I want to go?" Cactus Jack laughed. "Uh, yeah."

"It's yours then," Brooks said.

Cactus Jack roped him in for a quick hug. "Thanks, man."

Torpedo turned to her former roommate. "You want to be my date?"

Human Touch nodded. "Of course."

The group turned to Doctor Queer and Blanche.

"Sorry," Brooks said.

"I'm not that into it anyway," Blanche lied. Inside, she was longing for something to be a part of.

"Do not pity me," Doctor Queer said. "I can experience the performance via the astral plane. But we really should find Godwin before something happens to him."

"Absolutely," Cactus Jack said, "but..."

"He has magma powers," Brooks offered.

Torpedo agreed. "He has magma powers! He'll be fine."

"As many times as we've been delayed, what's another few hours?" Human Touch asked.

"Exactly," Brooks said. "We have until midnight. Traffic will be clear by the time we're done. It'll be *fine*."

"Worse comes to worst, we can take you up on that

teleportation," Torpedo said.

Doctor Queer sighed. "As you wish."

Torpedo clanked her gloves together to make sure everyone was paying attention. "Three hours to show time. Everyone go home, grab a bag of clothes to change into."

Cactus Jack grinned. "We'll reconvene after a brief recess?"

Torpedo gave him a high five for the *Hamilton* lyric. "We'll meet at the theater."

"I'm already wearing a suit," Brooks said.

Torpedo was quick to make a suggestion. "You could hang out with Percival for a few hours."

The group snickered.

"You can hang out with me 'n' the doc!" Blanche said.

"Quite," Doctor Queer said. "We could go over the Q.U.E.E.R. Method I was telling you about."

"Doubt he needs help with that," Cactus Jack said.

Brooks sighed.

Outside the Richard Rodgers Theater, Blanche sat in a damp alley with Doctor Queer's limp, lifeless body propped up against her shoulder. This was the price of astral projection, but it was worth it as he joined Brooks, Jack, Ana, and Abby inside. His teammates couldn't see him floating above the front row, but if they were going to insist on seeing the sold-out show instead of completing a rescue mission, he wasn't going to miss it.

Dressed in their civilian best, the Bedazzlers settled into their seats.

"This is exciting," Ana said. "I haven't seen a show since... ever."

"Never?" Abby asked.

"No," Ana said. "My parents don't approve, and I'm too poor to afford it on my own."

"Don't approve?" Abby wondered.

"She's—" Jack started.

Ana shot him a warning look.

"—She picked a hell of a first show," Jack said.

Is your view okay? Brooks asked.

My view is exactly the same as your view, Smith said.

"Hey!" Abby said to get everyone's attention. She sat on one end, and she raised her phone high to take a selfie of the four corporeal Bedazzlers. Doctor Queer's astral form leaned in, but it didn't make the shot.

"Tag me on that," Jack said.

Ana tapped his arm. "@TheHumanPorcupine?"

Everyone knew he was @HofstraLaw96, but they still laughed. Jack glowered.

"I thought you liked that she's breaking bad?" Abby asked.

"I did until now," Jack said.

Ana gestured at Brooks. "If you want, we can go back to making fun of him for sleeping with Percival."

Brooks muttered under his breath. *"Mira qué cabrón."*

"Uh oh. He's Spanish mad," Abby said.

Smith offered some virtual consolation. *I'd stand up for you, but... One: I don't exist. Two: I'm amped up for Hamilton right now. Three: it's still fucking hilarious to me.*

"Did you speak Spanish for Percival?" Jack asked.

"Oh, for—"

With no warning, the lights dimmed, the curtains drew, and the group shut up.

Three hours later, they emerged victorious, singing *Hamilton* lyrics as they caught up with Blanche and Doctor Queer. In what could not be described as a classy moment, the group undressed and began putting their costumes on behind an alley dumpster.

"How was it?" Blanche asked.

"Amazing," Jack said.

"Incredible," Abby said.

"Fantastic," Ana said.

"I'm not going to lie," Brooks said. "I liked it."

I told you, Smith said.

While he was out, Doctor Queer had drooled on Blanche's poncho. He came to, wiping his mouth. "I'm sorry."

"Don't worry about it," Blanche said. "But if you wanna make it up to me, I'd love to see the show some time."

Doctor Queer put a hand to his chin. "Hmm. I don't actually have a job, per se..."

Torpedo put on her last glove. "Hey, Hot Stuff. What time is it?"

"Five past eleven o'clock," Hot Stuff said.

"Shit," Torpedo said.

Cactus Jack eyed the line of taxis outside the theater. "I have an idea."

"What?" Torpedo asked.

"Why don't we take a cab? Well, two cabs."

"Good idea," Doctor Queer said.

"Let's," Brooks said.

"Perfect," Human Touch said.

Blanche would have taken credit for the idea that she'd had hours earlier, but everyone seemed so happy about it that she didn't want to sour the mood.

She shouted a useless "Let's go!" and the Bedazzlers were on their way.

25

FORCE

I t would make sense that a person capable of the methodical capture, disarmament, and murder of an entire superhero team would be patient, but the trucker was not, and he tapped a steel table with his fingers. He'd already built a tolerance to the Xanax prescribed in the wake of his daughter's sea-monstering, and he was anything but calm.

"Where are your friends?" he demanded.

"I told you. They're not coming," Monochrome said.

Monochrome was the only one in the room wearing a watch, but he couldn't check it for obvious reasons. Luckily, the trucker had gone through the trouble of buying a five-inch analog desk clock so his captives could hear its dramatic ticking.

11:58. One second passed. Then another. Then another. Just as forty-three more had done the same, the garage's metal door creaked open.

Blanche set foot inside first, wheezing. "We made it!"

The others rushed in after her.

"One minute and fourteen seconds left," Monochrome said. "*Really*?"

Torpedo shrugged. "I text—"

Monochrome gaped at Human Touch. "What in my name is on your face?"

"My new mask," she said.

Monochrome was heated. "You had time to visit the party

store, but you got here with *one minute and fourteen seconds left?*"

"Like I was saying," Torpedo said, "I texted you. We won *Hamilton* tickets."

"I didn't get a message. This douchebag destroyed my phone," Monochrome said.

The trucker stood up from his table and sneered. "Finally, the 'heroes' have arriv—"

"Wait." Monochrome cut him off. "You went to see *Hamilton* without me?"

"Uh, yeah," Torpedo said.

"Of course we did," Brooks said. "We don't like you."

"You came to rescue me—"

Brooks rocked his hand back and forth in an ehhh gesture.

"You're not allowed in the theater anyway," Torpedo said.

Monochrome glanced from Torpedo to Brooks and back. "You took *him?*"

"I went too," Human Touch said. She held a hand to her mask's mouth hole and, in a moment of great pride, successfully avoided gagging at the corpses littering the room.

The trucker couldn't get a sentence in. "—going to die... echoes of vengeance—"

"Me too," Cactus Jack said.

"I viewed the performance via the astral plane," Doctor Queer said.

Blanche deflated. "I didn't get to go."

Monochrome ignored her and continued complaining to Torpedo. "That could have been our date."

"Oh my God. She's not going to date you," Brooks said.

"She will for info on 1994," Monochrome said.

"What happened in 1994?" Cactus Jack asked.

"Ha! Like I'm going to tell you. That's for her to find out... on our date."

Torpedo rolled her eyes behind her faceplate.

The trucker cackled. "I know all about 1994. That was the year—"

"You shut your mouth," Monochrome snapped. Without warning, liquid metal began dripping onto his hair. He dropped a few inches to the floor, looked up, and saw that he'd unwittingly melted the pipe above himself. "Hey, look at that. Powers are back."

"Yeah, that drug doesn't work forever," the Immortal Man said. He tilted his head with a droll smile. "Did I forget to mention that?"

"It doesn't matter," the trucker said. "I'll still best you in comba—"

Monochrome raised a hand and shot a burst of magma across the room. It hit the trucker's chest, and he was dead in an instant. His body slumped to the floor in two melty pieces.

The Bedazzlers' jaws dropped.

"Dude," Cactus Jack said. "You just murdered that guy."

Monochrome spread his arms out, gesturing at the warehouse. "Uh, yeah. He killed all these people and was going to kill us. You're welcome."

"We agreed to abide by the law," Torpedo said.

"Yeah. Killing people in self-defense is totally legal," Monochrome said.

"That doesn't seem right," Blanche said.

"He did say we were all going to die..." Cactus Jack said.

Human Touch added, "And there are all the bodies proving he'll do it."

"Still," Cactus Jack said.

"Still," Torpedo said.

"Can someone let me down?" the Immortal Man asked.

Without looking, Monochrome threw a hand back over his shoulder and melted the end of the other pipe. The Immortal Man shimmied toward the new break in the pipe and dropped down onto the floor. Cactus Jack met him with a pair of handcuff keys taken from the steel table.

Monochrome, meanwhile, brushed some cooled bits of

metal out of his hair. They fell to the floor with a TINK TINK TINK. Human Touch tugged Brooks toward the billionaire and grabbed him by the wrist.

"How does killing another human being make you feel?" she asked.

Monochrome blinked. "HT, what are you doing?"

"How do you *feel?*" Human Touch repeated.

"Annoyed? You clearly don't have any control over your power yet." Monochrome turned to Brooks. "Take her back."

"No way. She turns me into a snippy asshole," Brooks said.

I don't think that's how it works, Smith said.

"It's *your* turn," Brooks insisted.

"I don't want a turn," Monochrome said. "She's all sweaty from seeing corpses."

Brooks took a deep breath. "Listen. I looked into the Mirror of Regret earlier, and I'm not in the mood to—"

The Immortal Man shuffled over. "I'll take her—"

BLAM! POW! POP!

As he reached a hand out, a bullet shot through his stomach. Blood splashed Human Touch's shirt as she leapt from Monochrome's arm and tackled Brooks to the floor. The other Bedazzlers followed her lead, dropping for cover.

"No you won't," a voice said from more shadows.

"*Obice invisibilia*," Doctor Queer said. With those words, an invisible forcefield formed around the team, deflecting dozens more incoming bullets. The bullets struck like drops of rain hitting a puddle, leaving visible, radiating circles of white that dissipated into nothing. Doctor Queer appeared to be fine, and before anyone could tell him that he appeared to be fine, he alerted them to the spell's effect. "I am now allergic to penicillin..."

"Who are these guys?" Human Touch asked. Their attackers remained tucked in the shadows, and neither she nor anyone else could see faces yet.

Monochrome had a more important question. "Why did you push Agent Brooks to the ground and not me?"

"I like him," Human Touch said.

Monochrome scowled. "*Honestly.* See if I kill someone for you next time."

"None of us wanted you to kill him," Torpedo said.

"You would have if you'd met the guy," Monochrome said. He jerked his head toward Brooks. "He doesn't care that I killed him."

Brooks, still holding Human Touch's hand, stood silent.

"That man probably had a family," Human Touch said.

"Yeah, about that. His wife was eaten by the sea monster," Monochrome said.

"That's *horrible*," Cactus Jack said.

"And his daughter *was* the sea monster, soooo—"

Cactus Jack's jaw dropped. "I choked someone's baby girl?"

Monochrome shrugged. "Someone's murderous little sea monster."

Cactus Jack put a hand over his mouth and slumped to the floor. "Oh my God."

Bullets continued bouncing off the side of the forcefield and hitting the floor with a PLINK PLINK PLINK.

"You couldn't have mentioned that this guy had backup before?" Torpedo asked.

"I didn't know he had any," Monochrome said.

"We're not his backup," an annoying voice said. "We're here to finish the job."

"Ugh. I know that voice," Torpedo said. "Traffic Jam?"

Sure enough, Traffic Jam stepped into the lit area, alongside Mal Licious, Sarah Daniels, Tecumseh Jackson, the three Webers, and Heidi Werewith. The Reticent board would have been entirely accounted for, but Arab Spring's pieces were melding back together in a subway station, and Travis Marsh had suffered a rough day of decay and had to be placed in an industrial refrigerator.

"You guys are using guns now?" Cactus Jack asked.

"They're doing whatever is necessary," Werewith said. She turned to the Webers. "Now. How do we get past this forcefield?"

Two of the Webers spoke at once. "It's a mystery."

"Oooh. Mystery," the third Weber echoed.

While the incompetent members of the Reticent board tapped at the forcefield, the Immortal Man was busy bleeding out. Blanche applied pressure to his stomach with her poncho. Brooks handed Human Touch off to Cactus Jack and knelt down next to the body.

"I thought this fellow was s'posed to be immortal," Blanche said.

"I knew he was overrated," Monochrome muttered.

"Not again," Brooks said, his voice noticeably softer. "I didn't think it applied to him too..."

"What are going you on about?" Monochrome asked.

Brooks snipped back a rhetorical question. "How did my husband die?"

"Oh. Ohhh," Monochrome said. "Yikes."

"I'm so sorry," Brooks said to the Immortal Man.

"I'm confused," Blanche said.

Cactus Jack agreed. "Me too."

"I killed him," Brooks said.

We've been over this. You did not—

"He's not dead yet," Blanche noted.

The Immortal Man, despite his gritted teeth and balmy face, nodded. "I don't think they hit any vital organs. I'll... be okay..."

"Not *him*." Brooks struggled to explain what had happened. "When they made me a cyborg, something went wrong and I kind of... drain immortality. Eddie wasn't supposed to be able to die, but..."

"Oh," Blanche said. "Ohhh."

"Harsh," Cactus Jack said.

Brooks gestured at the not-so-Immortal Man. "So now he's going to die because of me too."

"Or you could, you know, *step away from him*," Monochrome said.

Torpedo snapped at him. "We're in a forcefield, jackass."

Even if they hadn't been in the middle of a forcefield, Brooks wouldn't have been able to move. Crippling anxiety slumped him to the ground, and he stared at the metal-baring hole in his forearm.

"Fuck, fuck, fuck," he said, burying his head in his hands.

Outside the protective bubble, Heidi Werewith chuckled. "If nothing else, it will be easy to get *that* piece of stolen property back."

Monochrome waved a hand in front of the cyborg's face. "Hyello?"

Hey, remember the Q.U.E.E.R. Method? Smith asked. *Now would be a great time for you to get really—*

Brooks sneered. *The first step is quiet, and we're being shot at while the Immortal Man is dying.*

Doctor Queer resolved to fix things. With one arm still raised, holding up the forcefield, he used the other to heal the Immortal Man's wound. He pointed at one of the angry gunmen, and the wound reappeared on that man's torso instead. A single Weber dropped to the floor.

"Evil," the two unshot Webers said, gasping.

"Evil," the shot one choked out after them.

The Immortal Man sat up. "Thanks."

"Are we all killing people now?" Torpedo asked.

"He'll live," Doctor Queer said. "Just as the Immortal Man would have. I'm trying to calm our teammate." He gestured at Brooks.

Smith tried to do the same. *Babe. Come here.*

"I am *always* here. You're in my head *because I killed you*."

"I think your wires are crossed there," Monochrome said.

He made a mental note to bring someone with actual medical experience onto the team next time... or maybe computer experience... or experience with anything useful.

You're getting your conversations mixed up. Come here, Smith said.

In the real world, a taco bar is a great place to catch whatever disease has been sneezed into the meat trays by pestilent patrons. In The Afterlife™, Brooks and Smith had been enjoying the perfectly hygienic Taco Bar scenario. That was no longer the case, as virtual Brooks pushed his plate to the floor and slumped over a diner booth. Smith prodded his arm and looked up at the restaurant's TV, which displayed reality.

He's fine, Smith said. *Doctor Poof took care of it.*

Brooks despaired. *You're not.*

Sure I am. We've got the best taco bar in the world, Smith said. He moved around to the other side of the booth and scooted in. Brooks didn't respond to that, so Smith began rubbing his shoulders.

Brooks responded to that with some incoherent mumbles, so Smith kept figuring things out for himself. *I share your senses. If I can hear what you hear and I can pop into your dreams, why can't I hijack your body?*

What—?

Stay here, Smith said. *Quiet's the first step. Pop into the Desert Oasis. I'm gonna hijack your body for a few minutes.*

That sounds like something you shouldn't do.

In the real world, he did. Brooks's body stood, stumbled a little, walked over to Monochrome, and wrapped two pissed-off cyborg hands around his neck.

Smith spoke through him. "You're gonna *get me out of here.*"

He loosened his grip and Monochrome choked out a reply. "What?"

"I don't care if you put me in a robot or a talking dog. You're gonna get me out of here."

"Agent Smith?" Monochrome made a huh sound. "That's new."

Blanche whispered to Cactus Jack. "A talking dog would be *adorable*." He nodded in agreement.

Torpedo groaned at Monochrome and Smith. "Could you two not fight for three seconds? We're surrounded!"

They could not. The cyborg hands tightened their grip again, and Monochrome pulled at them with his own. A light glow caused Smith to pull Brooks's body away, lest it lose more skin to magma.

Monochrome coughed. "Asshole."

Smith leaned in close. "Listen to me, you ashy fuck. This bullshit is killing him, and getting me out of here is something I know you can do. He's helped you more than enough, so if you don't do it, I'll find a way out of here myself, and I'll kill you."

"You don't kill people," Monochrome said.

"I haven't *yet*," Smith said, "but apparently it's the thing to do around here."

Eddie, Brooks said. *I'm fine.*

"You're not fine," Smith said.

"Excuse me?" Monochrome asked.

See? It's hard to keep up with two conversations, Brooks said.

While the non-shot members of the Reticent board continued giving the forcefield useless taps and gunshots, Monochrome took to taunting them.

"You can't get in here," he said. "Our guy's better than your guys."

Doctor Queer shook his head.

Werewith crossed her arms. "We know you have a mage. That's why we found one for ourselves."

"Hmm?" Monochrome wondered.

An opaque black cloud moved in overhead and enveloped the forcefield.

"Well, that's not good," Monochrome said.

The Bedazzlers' last bit of light disappeared as the cloud reached the ground. Human Touch ducked behind Cactus

Jack's back.

"Get ready to fight, guys," Torpedo said.

26

SOMETHING MEMORABLE

The cloud that surrounded the Bedazzlers did not have a silver lining. If it were lined with any metal, it would have been pewter—heavy, dull, and enjoyed by people dressed entirely in black. Doctor Queer knew in an instant what brand of evil had surrounded his forcefield.

"Percival," he sneered.

No one could see the dread Percival, but they heard him cackle.

"This is why you kill your nemeses," Monochrome said.

"A truck driver with PTSD was *not your nemesis*," Smith said.

"Percival?" Torpedo wondered. "I thought you were done being evil."

"Yeah," Human Touch said. "What about Times Square?"

"What about Elmo?" Cactus Jack added.

No one could see Percival's frown as he spoke with a low voice. "Those eerie triplets gave Elmo some cocaine cut with rat poison. They threatened to do the same to Buzz Leapyear if I didn't agree to help them."

Smith tried to correct him on the character's name, but Percival ignored him and spoke to Doctor Queer. "In any case, *doctor*. I still hate you, so I agreed."

If smirks were audible, that's what Werewith's voice sounded like as she spoke. "We also told him we'd give him a shot with the robot before we take it back."

"Fuck off. This body's mine to use, not yours," Smith said.

Wow, Brooks said.

Percival sighed. "And *I* told *them* it's not really worth a second go."

Well, Brooks said. *I feel great about myself...*

Smith counted facts on his fingers. "One: He's not an it. Two: He's *definitely* worth a second go. Three: If you dragged the entire Reticent board all the way to Coney Island, he's obviously worth a lot."

"You think we came all the way out here for him... er, you?" Werewith asked.

"Well, yeah. All that shit about taking back your property," Smith said.

"As a *bonus*," Werewith said.

"Then why did you come here?" Torpedo asked.

Werewith pointed at Monochrome. "To ensure *he dies*."

The black cloud still hung around the forcefield, so nobody knew where she was pointing.

"Who?" Cactus Jack asked.

Percival corrected the problem. "*Noctis Magica... Videre!*"

Mal Licious frowned and kicked at the ground as her favorite color faded and the black cloud transformed into a grey, translucent one.

"That's better," Percival said.

The view outside the forcefield was foggy, but Monochrome stepped toward the purplish figure. "Why did you make it black in the first place?"

"For the aesthetic," Percival said.

Monochrome nodded. "Well, I can appreciate that."

Werewith pointed at Monochrome again. "In any case, it's him. We're here to kill *him*." She glanced at her own board members. "These idiots were *supposed* to stop you from getting here and rescuing him. Then whatshisface with the goatee would kill Monochrome at midnight. It was perfect."

Human Touch gasped. "We didn't really win *Hamilton* tickets."

Werewith slow-clapped. "We rigged the lottery."

"You coulda rigged it so three of us won," Blanche said. "Geez."

"That would have been unrealistic. You'd have figured out it was a sham."

Monochrome sighed. "What did I ever do to you?"

"Oh, I don't know," Werewith said. "Mysterious interference at City Hall?"

"Oh. That's right." Monochrome chuckled.

Werewith raised her voice. "You *forgot*? Our lives have been hell trying to rebuild our company and you *forgot* you were doing it?"

Torpedo stared at Monochrome. "What could you possibly need from them that you resorted to—?"

"Real estate," Cactus Jack said. "He wants their property. I've done some of the paperwork."

"I don't *want* it," Monochrome corrected. "I want them to build it out so it looks *nice*. I have to see their disgusting lot from my office, you know."

Blanche squinted. "We have enemies 'cause you didn't like the look of a building?"

"*Apparently*," Monochrome said. He coughed on a plume of smoke seeping into the forcefield from above.

Human Touch eyed him, then the Webers facing her with their guns drawn. "It's eating away at our forcefield. Does anyone have a plan yet?"

"Stand back," Doctor Queer said.

"Great plan. Thank you," Smith said.

Torpedo eyed him. "*God*. You're even saltier than Brooks."

"I'm *dead*," Smith noted.

You were salty even when you were alive, Brooks said.

The dread Percival waved his hands around, their contortion even more convoluted than Doctor Queer's. His middle and ring fingers crossed while his pointer and thumb made a loop. His pinkies stretched as far as they could to run perpendicular to the rest. He responded to Smith's statement in a booming voice. "Soon you'll all be dead!"

Monochrome dusted his sleeve. "Can I melt *him*?"

"No," Torpedo and Cactus Jack said.

Tecumseh knelt down to ready his musket. While he was making all of the preparations necessary to fire, everything that follows happened...

The Bedazzlers' bubble burst in an implosion of grey smoke, and there was a rush to hide behind Torpedo's armor. Bullets bounced off her with a TING TING TING as Doctor Queer's hands glowed chartreuse.

"*Telum vale!*" he said.

The most imminent threat—the Webers' guns—disappeared, and Doctor Queer doubled over in a severe coughing fit, the natural consequence of their disarmament.

"Go, go, go!" Torpedo said. She flew forward and tackled Percival as the other Bedazzlers ran toward the two healthy Webers, Traffic Jam, and Mal Licious. The Immortal Man, being mortal at the time, took her words at face value and walked out of the building to take a cab home.

"Good luck," he said with a wave.

Percival began a spell of his own. "*Noctis Magica, omnis—*"

"No," Torpedo said, covering his mouth.

HURGUR CECK HECK. Doctor Queer hacked and choked and mumbled through his hacking and choking. "Not going... work..." CHECK HACK BLER.

Percival waved a hand for some wordless magic, and Torpedo flew backward, away from him. "Did you really think my skills are so petty they require speech?"

"If you don't have to say stuff, why do it?" Human Touch asked.

"Again, for the aesthetic."

Monochrome nodded along.

Percival, meanwhile, threw back his cape and made a declaration for the Bedazzlers. "I will fight none but the Divine

Dimensionmaster!"

TURGRUFFF HACK SHLEP. Doctor Queer nodded.

They moved to one corner of the room to handle their rivalry. As woo-woo, sparkly magic blew around the room, Torpedo sized up the situation.

"We just have to handle one old woman, two of the creepy triplets, Traffic Jam, and that weird Goth lady." Her voice took a smug turn. "And none of them have guns."

That wasn't strictly true, as Tecumseh was still readying his musket, but no one paid him any mind.

Monochrome laughed. "How ever will we handle these people we've already defeated?"

"You guys are outnumbered, and Arch *always* beats Percival," Torpedo said. "Give up."

"Outnumbered?" a Weber asked with a gleam in one of his mismatched eyes.

"You just fucking jinxed it," Smith said.

Cactus Jack scoffed. "You don't believe in superstitions, do—"

A knock at the door shut him up.

"That should be our backup," Werewith said.

"Backup?" Human Touch asked from behind Cactus Jack.

While "backup" normally indicates a Plan B, the group that pushed through the warehouse door should have been Plan A. The re-formed (but not reformed) Arab Spring stepped into the building first, followed by no fewer than sixteen Webers. No one could get an accurate count because they all looked the same. It still wasn't clear whether they were aliens, clones, or some new species of monster, but it was clear they were not triplets. At the tail end of the party was none other than the grotesque transformation of Doug Daniels—Aisle 9. His wife Sarah had given him a new list, and he shouted it with fury.

"MERNERCREM. TERPERDER. CERCTURS JERK. HERMAN TERCH. ARGEN BERKS. DERCTER

KWER."

Blanche rolled her hand in a go-on gesture, but the monster was finished. She sighed. "I'm not even on the bad guys' radar? Cripes."

"Can I melt them?" Monochrome asked.

"No," several of the team said at once.

"No killing," Cactus Jack said. "We'll just... wear them down."

"Ugh. *Fine.*"

"I don't care if you kill them," Smith said.

Torpedo lowered her faceplate so she could glower at him. "Outvoted."

Human Touch looked to Torpedo. "If you could handle the giant monster, that would be good."

"I could melt it," Monochrome said.

"No," everyone said again.

Instead of magmatizing anyone, Monochrome shot tiny bits of magma at the ground and let them cool into rocks. He began picking them up and tossing them at Webers, one by one. Basalt is lightweight and perfect for landscaping, but makes an imperfect projectile. The rocks did very little.

"Stop that," a Weber said.

"Stop," the others repeated.

A piece hit Traffic Jam in the face, leaving a dusty black mark on his pasty forehead. The ginger terror complained. "You're just being annoying."

"Oh, you'd know." Monochrome tossed another rock.

While Monochrome and Traffic Jam bickered, Arab Spring had a grudge of his own.

"*You,*" he sneered.

"Me?" Blanche asked, pointing at herself.

Arab Spring nodded. "You're going to pay."

Blanche didn't say anything, but under the balaclava she formed a huge grin.

I have a nemesis, she thought. *I'm a real hero.*

Arab Spring bounced toward Blanche, ready to punish her for dodging him earlier and getting him hit by a subway train. She dodged again and—anticipating his bounce—whipped around to face the other direction.

"Sorry," she said, pulling up just enough balaclava to reveal a bit of her neck.

Arab Spring missed her on the rebound and flattened against the ground in a panic.

"I can't see," he said, palming at concrete. "I can't see!"

"I'm sorry," Blanche said. "You tried to kill me, though."

Arab Spring stood and jerked his head around, trying to hear the action. "You're going to pay for this. You're all going to pay!"

With that, the spring-man began springing around the room with no goal in sight. Everyone—Bedazzlers and Webers alike—was forced to keep an eye out for his bizarre bounding.

Monochrome knelt to pick up some more rocks and dodged a bounce in the process. "This just went from bad to worse *again*. Thanks, Blanche."

The warehouse filled with the sounds of Zanium blasts, twinkly magic bursts, fisticuffs, Webers echoing over each other, and an agitated spring bouncing from wall to wall complaining about life's unfairness. But none of that was audible to Brooks as he worked through the Q.U.E.E.R. Method in the Desert Oasis scenario. While Smith did the battling—he had more of a taste for it anyway—Brooks sat cross-legged on the sand.

Step One (Quiet) came easily. Step Two (Unhappiness) was a bit trickier. Not because Brooks couldn't think of anything that made him unhappy, but because he could think of too many things. The cyborg thing... the brain sharing... the superhero blackmail... all of it boiled down to his life being a tremendous clusterfuck he'd prefer it not be.

Step Three (Exoneration). When it came down to it, and

Brooks asked himself what he could have done differently for any of those things to change, the answer was nothing. He hadn't made himself a cyborg, he hadn't asked to share his brain with a dead man, he hadn't asked for immortality-sucking powers, and—going all the way back to when he got started in paranormal detecting—he hadn't done anything to provoke monsters into attacking his family. Despite the logic, one nagging thought remained. He called for his husband.

Little busy here, Smith said, tossing a Weber across the room.

Is there any way I could have... I don't know... convinced you not to kill yourself?

Well, it was an accident, so no. Smith returned to his old standby: *Hamilton* lyrics. *Let me tell you what I wish I'd known—*

Oh, goddamn it, Brooks said.

Step Four (Empowerment). Brooks accepted Smith's answer and, with it, that he had done everything he could. There were no other billionaires offering faint promises of a robot body. There were no others with the ability to create a cyborg instruction manual. Sure, his wagon was hitched to a disastrous super team, but it was the only wagon he had. His circumstances were as under his control as they could be, which was not at all.

It was time for Step Five (Release). He called out again.

Still busy, Smith said, dodging a Weber and letting it crash into another Weber.

Too busy for a 1912 Renault?

"I'll be right back," Smith said, stepping away from the battle.

"What the—" Monochrome's objection was cut off by the sound of the warehouse door shutting.

With Doctor Queer and Agent Smith preoccupied, the Bedazzlers were left with five members to face the onslaught.

Torpedo hit Aisle 9 with Zanium ray after Zanium ray, to no effect. "Why are there so many of these freaks?"

"Freaks," all the Webers said at once. It was freaky.

As Human Touch and Cactus Jack twirled around, dodging Webers, she tapped his shoulder. "I could try the thing. I have a feeling it might work."

"A *feeling*?" Cactus Jack asked.

"I'll keep blasting him as a distraction," Torpedo said.

She did that, and Aisle 9 tried to swat at her as Cactus Jack and Human Touch walked hand-in-hand to the monster's back.

"Up you go," Cactus Jack said, giving her a boost.

Human Touch wrapped her arms around the creature's neck and dangled. "You don't actually want to hurt anyone, do you?"

Aisle 9 stomped and ranted. "MERNERCREM. TERPERDER. CERCTURS JERK. HERMAN TERCH. ARGEN BERKS. DERCTER KWER."

"But they all helped you before," Human Touch said. "You know that."

"MERNERCREM... TERPERDER..."

"Do you want to hurt me?" she asked.

"NER... ERJUSWERNER GERDASTER ANERBUR TERMPERNS."

Monochrome stopped tossing rocks for a moment to express confusion. "*What?*"

"You can go to the store," Human Touch said, "and you don't have to buy tampons if you don't want to."

"NER?"

"You control your own life," Human Touch said.

"It doesn't seem like he does," Monochrome said, "being crazy susceptible to following lists and all..."

Human Touch ignored her team's leader and repeated herself for Aisle 9. "You control your own life."

"HMM."

Aisle 9 shrank back into Doug Daniels. The underwear-clad man glanced over at his wife, who was slapping

Monochrome in the face, and then back at the door.

"I'm going to the store," Doug said, "and I'm not bringing a list."

Monochrome threw a rock at him. "Go. No one cares."

SLAPP. Sarah got him again.

Monochrome rolled his eyes and huffed.

A creak signaled the reopening of the warehouse door. On his way out, Doug bumped Agent Smith, who strutted into the room. "What did I miss?"

"I defeated the monster," Human Touch said.

Cactus Jack patted her on the back.

"Don't say it like that," Monochrome said. "'Defeat' sounds way more impressive than 'convinced him to leave.'"

"Sorry we don't all *melt* our problems," Cactus Jack said.

Monochrome lit up. "Magma gun!"

"What?" Cactus Jack asked.

"If I invent a magma gun, you can."

"We don't wanna kill anyone," Blanche said.

As the Bedazzlers continued bickering, Human Touch sighed. "Some moment of glory."

"Don't get too excited, Zane," Torpedo said. "There's plenty of Webers where he came from."

There were more than enough Webers, approaching in formation, and the sight of them put a bad taste in the Bedazzlers' mouths—a taste worse than the beef stock they were all tasting thanks to Mal Licious. She leaned against a wall in the back of the room and smirked at the thought of invading their taste buds.

As Monochrome, Torpedo, Smith, Cactus Jack, and Human Touch tried to handle the Webers, Doctor Queer and Percival caused a ruckus. A purple blast of something grazed Cactus Jack's face, and his cheek felt a sudden, nearly unbearable coldness.

"Could you watch where you're blasting?" he asked.

"My apologies," Doctor Queer said through a sneeze.

Blanche wasn't fighting in any way that made sense, and Torpedo, flying above the action, noticed. While the Bedazzlers and the Reticent faced each other, zapping and punching away, Blanche weaved back and forth in the middle of the warehouse, circling one crate in particular. Every once in a while, she leaned down to look under it. Torpedo realized what was going on when a tiny orange tail popped out from underneath the crate.

Tecumseh rose from the ground and took aim at Cactus Jack, which everyone judged to be a little racist. Then he spoke. "The North shall rise again! I'm going to liberate you." Everyone found that part *extremely* racist. The thing sounded like a cannon, and its BOOOOM echoed throughout the warehouse. His gun more aimless than the average Millennial, Tecumseh's bullet flew nowhere near Cactus Jack. It launched toward Blanche. In the mixed commotion of Doctor Queer and Percival's magic and the bouncing Arab Spring, it was impossible to tell exactly what had hit her, but she yelped and crumpled to the ground.

Torpedo suppressed a beef bouillon-induced urge to vomit and resolved to remove the thing that had distracted Blanche.

"Hot Stuff," Torpedo said. "Amplify my voice."

"As you wish," Hot Stuff said.

"*WAIT!*" Torpedo shouted.

The entire room—heroes, villains, and those in between—stopped what they were doing. For the Bedazzlers, it was a welcome breather. Cactus Jack and Doctor Queer weren't in great shape, Human Touch was quite tired of running around being tossed from hand to hand, and Monochrome only ever worked out his vanity muscles. They hacked and wheezed as Torpedo walked over to the crate and pulled a kitten from underneath it. She stepped out of the warehouse for a moment to unleash it. When she came back inside, she shut the door behind herself, ensuring it would remain safely outside.

Monochrome, meanwhile, gave Blanche's face a slap. "Blanche?"

"Is she okay?" Torpedo asked.

It didn't look promising. Blanche's chest was half-collapsed and covered in blood. Monochrome removed one of her gloves and shielded his eyes to feel her pulse. There wasn't one.

He slid the glove back on. "Uh, she's dead."

"Are you sure?" Human Touch asked.

"I just killed a guy," Monochrome said. "I'm sure."

The rest of the team gathered around her as the Reticent board stood and shuffled their feet.

"What are you waiting for?" Werewith asked. "Kill them while they're mourning."

"Kill?" Traffic Jam asked. "When did we get to killing?"

"Have you been paying attention? At all?"

"There's no honor in killing a foe who isn't fighting back," Percival said. Waiting for the inevitable, uncomfortable display of human emotion to pass so he could kill Doctor Queer, he pulled out his phone for a quick round of Hokeyblock Blast. Tecumseh, meanwhile, knelt to the ground to prepare his next shot.

Torpedo removed her faceplate. "Oh my God."

"I can't believe she's gone," Human Touch said, her eyes wide in shock.

"She was the best of us," Monochrome said.

Smith offered a rapid blink. "Wait... what?"

"We have to win this for her," Cactus Jack said.

"For Blanche," Monochrome said.

Everyone but Smith echoed him with gusto. "For Blanche!"

Smith offered an even more rapid blink. "*What?*"

The worn and beaten Bedazzlers stood tall with newfound energy. They dusted themselves off, prepared to win this battle.

They all shouted again. "For Blanche!"

Smith was unimpressed. He turned to Monochrome. "You didn't like Blanche. You couldn't even bother giving her a costume or a code name."

"Don't speak ill of the dead," Doctor Queer said. "It's unbecoming."

"Are you fucking kidding me?" Smith said.

She's dead, Brooks said. *Show some respect.*

I'm the only one who finds this weird? Smith asked.

I want my body back. You're making me look callous.

Fine.

"Rest in peace, Blanche," Brooks said from his own body.

Human Touch wiped away some tears. "She never even got to see *Hamilton*."

Torpedo repeated her with a softer voice. "She never got to see *Hamilton*."

Cactus Jack stood and let his tears flow freely. "For Blanche!"

"For Blanche!" the Bedazzlers said.

In spite of the rallying cry, the Bedazzlers' abilities did not change. They were no more capable of rallying than they had been before Blanche died. Things only got worse for them.

Rather than spending the night bickering with Monochrome, Traffic Jam made his abilities useful by rapidly alternating the room's colors. Lights, walls, and costumes went from pink to blue to green to white and every other color. Everyone squinted and groaned as the warehouse took on the look and feel of a rave.

Brooks pressed at his temples and pleaded to Traffic Jam. "Can you stop with the lights?"

"Why would he stop?" Werewith asked. "It's working. We're wearing you down."

Percival's senses were better than a human being's, and the lights bothered him more than anyone. "I tire of this battle. *Noctis Magica... Non volant!*"

Doctor Queer, Torpedo, and Arab Spring all crashed to the floor. Unable to see anything or exact revenge, Arab Spring curled into a ball and began sobbing.

"You're all grounded," Percival said. "And now, Archibald, you will watch your friends die before you."

Cactus Jack turned to Human Touch. "You want to try the thing?"

"Might as well," she said.

They ran over and Human Touch grabbed Percival's arm.

He beat her to the punch. "Oh, I'm afraid not. *Noctis Magica... Verum!*"

A wave of black magic radiated from Percival's body, knocking everyone in the warehouse over. Human Touch fell backward into Cactus Jack's arms.

"I'm a lesbian—" she said. No one cared.

"—and Mormon." Everyone but Blanche and Cactus Jack exchanged looks of terror.

Human Touch realized what had happened: the magician had turned her ability around on them. Her voice finally figured out how to emphasize words as she shouted at Percival. "Hey! Not cool."

"Sometimes I wish my mom would just pass already," Cactus Jack said. Then he realized what he'd said, and frowned.

"I often wish the same for myself," Doctor Queer said. "The path of the Divine Dimensionmaster is a lonely one."

Even from behind a faceplate where no one could see her look of shame, Torpedo's confession was an embarrassing one. "I don't mind Monochrome."

Before he had the chance to grin, Monochrome confessed. "That trucker wasn't the first guy I killed. There was an incident at boarding school, and my parents managed to pin it on my friend Ricky."

Torpedo's voice lit up way more than it should have at murder. "1994?"

Monochrome nodded and then glowered at Percival.

The Bedazzlers stared at Brooks.

Monochrome spoke for all of them. "You're not going to say anything revelatory?"

Brooks shook his head. "I guess the Q.U.E.E.R. Method really does work."

Human Touch stifled a laugh. "It didn't save you from Percival last time."

The Webers had no secrets to reveal either. They all rose at once, stood still, and stared at Percival as if awaiting orders. It was unsettling, and when all their heads tilted to the left at once, it became more so. They marched forward with renewed focus, and each Bedazzler was soon swarmed by three or more Webers. The creatures did not strike with fists or elbows, but with their tongues.

Monochrome found himself at the bottom of a pile of the sickly beings, with one licking his cheek. "Aaaaaaagh. Can I melt them now?"

"No," everyone said.

A Weber reached for Torpedo's faceplate, trying to tear it off. She shoved it away. "What are they doing? Do their tongues do anything, or is this just some weird kink?"

"Nobody knows, but it's working," Werewith grinned.

"Sorry," Monochrome said, "but this won't do." He pressed his agitated hands against the closest Weber's shoulder, and it scurried away, clutching burned skin. A few other Webers took steps back. "Yeah. I'll melt you." He pointed at the Webers harassing his teammates. "All of you. Leave them alone, or you'll get the magma."

"Magma," the Webers said.

"*You'll* be getting the musket," Tecumseh said. He rose to aim at Monochrome, but there was a rustling noise across the room and he turned. The orange kitten had somehow made its way back into the warehouse, and Tecumseh was disgusted. "Varmint!"

Torpedo and Cactus Jack emitted drawn-out noises that

almost sounded like the word no.

For Monochrome, this was a PR gift. It occurred to him that PR was everything—not just to the outside world, but also within the team. Torpedo was watching, and she was a bleeding heart vegetarian, already on edge from the artificial beef flavoring. Hot Stuff was recording. Monochrome looked toward her, smirked, and leapt toward the kitten, seemingly unconcerned that he was about to be hit with the same type of musket ball that had just killed Blanche.

For Doctor Queer, time seemed to slow. He didn't know what was going on in Godwin Zane's mind, only that he was about to offer a heroic sacrifice. His friend, he thought, had finally grown, and this, along with a sacrifice of his own, was enough to support some extremely powerful magic. Percival's jaw dropped as Doctor Queer waved his hands.

"*Violentiam prohibere!*"

Just as it would have struck Monochrome, the musket ball disappeared. A Weber who had begun licking Torpedo's ear fell to the ground.

"Well, then," Percival announced. "I suppose I'm going back to the time square."

Werewith stomped toward him and threw a fit. "You can't. We'll kill Buzz Leapyear."

Percival grinned. "You can't."

With those words, Percival vanished in a poof of smoke.

"I'm confused," Human Touch said.

"Me too," Cactus Jack said.

Torpedo knelt down to check on Doctor Queer, who was lying on the ground. "Are you okay? What did you do?"

"It's a binding spell," Doctor Queer said. "None of these villains will be able to harm another human being again." He tried to stand up but couldn't. "Oh, dear."

"What's the cost?" Brooks asked.

"It's supposed to be a human sacrifice, but I suppose Godwin's—"

"Codename," Monochrome said.

"—I suppose *Monochrome* jumping in front of the kitten counted as half a sacrifice, so I only had to give half of one myself." He tapped at his leg. "I cannot feel that."

"*Half* a sacrifice?" Brooks stared at him, bewildered. "You can't make *half* a sacrifice."

"Apparently one can," Doctor Queer said.

"Why would you sacrifice yourself?" Monochrome asked.

"It is my duty to care for this world before myself," Doctor Queer said.

"*I* wanted to sacrifice *myself* to save the day. You ruined it!"

"You're upset that I saved you?" Doctor Queer asked.

"Yes." Monochrome motioned toward Torpedo. "She was going to be impressed and fall in love with me."

"But you'd be dead," Doctor Queer said.

"Someone like me doesn't just die," Monochrome said. "I'd get revived or *something*."

"Wow," Brooks said.

Torpedo grabbed Monochrome's arm. "You're losing the few points you just got. Shut up."

Monochrome raised an eyebrow. "I got a few points?"

The disgruntled Reticent crew filed out the door, one by one. Traffic Jam guided Arab Spring, and a trio of Webers carried their injured Weber comrade. Heidi Werewith attempted to shake her fist at the Bedazzlers, but even that had been deemed too violent by the spell. She settled for a stern look.

Torpedo and Brooks, meanwhile, hoisted the paralyzed doctor onto their shoulders.

"I still know magic," Doctor Queer said. "I could choose to float."

"No one wants to smell that," Cactus Jack said.

"I can't believe I'm going to say this," Brooks said, "but you should probably magmatize the evidence of you killing that trucker."

"Definitely," Monochrome said. "And we're going to be extra careful about editing Hot Stuff's footage of tonight."

"So we're all good with spoliation of evidence now?" Cactus Jack asked.

"I wouldn't say we're good with it," Torpedo said, "but one bad guy died and one of us died. Zane's never going to magmatize anyone to death again." She turned to Monochrome. "Right?"

"Sure. Whatever you say." Monochrome raised his hands and pointed at the half-melted trucker. With a little concentration, a magma blast burned the two halves, and there was nothing left on the ground but a small mound of rock.

Cactus Jack took a step back to stay as far from Human Touch as he could. To his surprise, she didn't puke, gag, or even raise her hand to her mouth.

"Two of the Webers licked me," she said. "Nothing could ever be that bad."

That sounds like another jinx, Smith said.

27

PR IS EVERYTHING

Outside the warehouse, news vans backed up for blocks. Each one had to get footage of the Horse Whisperer dangling in front of the building, especially now that he'd been hanging there so long that birds had picked the meat away from one of his arms. News crews filed in and out of the warehouse, bumping into police officers as they came as close to the CRIME SCENE—DO NOT CROSS tape as they could.

A stretcher emerged, covered in a white sheet, and the Bedazzlers bowed their heads to pay respects to Blanche. One of the nearby anchors shoved a microphone into Monochrome's face to ask for some words on the matter. At first, he obliged.

"Once again, the day is saved, thanks to—" Monochrome watched as his teammates all cringed in fear of what he would say next. "—Actually, I'm not the team leader anymore. You should ask Torpedo."

She whispered to him. "What?"

"I said I'll do 'whatever you say,'" Monochrome said. "Was that not clear? You tell us what to do, and I'll do what you want, and you'll fall madly in love with me."

Torpedo stepped up to the microphones, stunned. "Well, we'll be cooperating with authorities and releasing the video of what happened tonight soon enough. Until then, the Bedazzlers will offer no comment."

"No comment?" Monochrome asked. "*No comment?* I change my mind."

Torpedo stepped away from the microphones and corralled him in for a whisper. "I already leaked the kitten part on YouTube."

"Is she really the team leader now?" Cactus Jack asked. Standing on his shoulder, the kitten rubbed against the side of his face.

"Sure," Monochrome said. "Whatever. It gives me more free time to work on other things."

"Like robot bodies?" Brooks asked.

"No. I had a lot of time to think in there. My next big thing is pep talk chapstick—"

The pair overheard a reporter, which prematurely ended their bickering. "Details are still emerging, but it's believed that the man who murdered Defense Squad Z and kidnapped Monochrome and the Immortal Man was a truck driver from New Jersey named Guy Napolillo. It's believed that he recruited several followers, still to be identified, for the purpose of causing grave harm to empowered humans. Guy himself seems to have escaped, but not before one last horrific act: endangering a kitten. Leaked footage believed to be from a security camera inside the warehouse shows Godwin Zane heroically throwing himself in front of a kitten that one of Guy's lackeys was preparing to shoot."

The internet lost its mind, and the Bedazzlers savored their trek back to the Bedazzlestation. #Bedazzlers, #Kitten, and #MyHeroes were among the top ten trending topics in the nation for hours. As they boarded the seatrain, one member of the team found this confusing.

"Let me get this straight," Brooks said.

Monochrome laughed. "You can't get anything straight."

Brooks ignored the comment and continued. "We stopped a monster destroying a grocery store..."

"Yep," Torpedo said.

"We stopped a dangerous traffic jam..."

"Yep."

"We defeated a sea monster..."

"Yep."

"All of those things made us less popular."

"Mmhmm."

Brooks pointed at Monochrome. "—but rescuing *you* from superpowered people *you* pissed off in the first place somehow gets us good PR."

"Don't forget the kitten," Human Touch said.

"It's really all about the kitten," Cactus Jack said, petting the tiny critter on his lap.

Torpedo nodded. "PR works in mysterious ways sometimes."

"It's not mysterious," Monochrome said. "Everything went exactly as I'd hoped."

"Um," Human Touch said. "Blanche *died*."

28

REBRANDED AGAIN

Unlike the Bedazzlers, every member of the Reticent board made it away from Coney Island alive. The only wounded Weber sat with a HealWrap™ around its torso, while the others suffered only minor bumps and bruises. Thanks to Doctor Queer's spell, they could do no physical harm, but it occurred to at least one member of the team that they never managed to do any in the first place.

"We weren't very good at supervillainy," Arab Spring said.

Mal Licious shook her head. "We really weren't."

Werewith shot them a chastising look. "We were never supervillains. If anyone asks, we were researching 'superhero alternatives.'"

Traffic Jam was puzzled. "Superhero alternatives?"

"Who's going to believe that?" Sarah asked.

"Have you *met* the public?" Werewith waved dismissively.

Travis Marsh, whose legs had rotted off, spoke from inside a laundry cart. "Why did you brrrraaaaaaai—bring us here?" A fly buzzed around his head, but no one could swat it.

"I have a new idea for putting this company back on track," Werewith said.

"What's that?" Sarah asked.

"We're going to sell insurance."

The Weber triplets shared a wicked laugh.

"Finally," one said. "Evil."

"Evil," the other two whispered at once.

Somewhere in New Jersey, the rest of the Webers cackled from within an abandoned house, and a passing jogger was struck with a sudden chill.

Werewith explained further. "With all you superpowered freaks out there, things are going to keep getting destroyed. I've come to an agreement with Godwin Zane. We'll offer insurance, and citizens who've been wronged will make claims with us instead of suing him."

"And he'll stop influencing City Hall to keep dicking with the permits?" Arab Spring asked.

"Well—" Werewith started. Her voice showed there was clearly another catch.

"Come *on*," Sarah said.

"We'll be permitted to build underground. The man has a weird thing about preserving the area's aesthetics, and frankly, with the performance you people just gave, we are in no place to argue."

"What's going above ground?" Traffic Jam asked.

"A Defense Squad Z memorial."

"Zane's putting in a monument to someone other than himself?" Sarah asked.

"Something about PR," Werewith said. "I don't know, and I don't care."

29

CARTE BLANCHE

With Blanche dead, every member of the Bedazzlers knew how to dress for a formal occasion. In this case, it was her funeral on Staten Island. The audience on this surprisingly sunny day was mostly comprised of a dozen or so distant aunts, uncles, and cousins who didn't know Blanche well enough to say anything about her. None of the Bedazzlers had much to offer either, but nothing could stop Godwin Zane from speaking.

He eyed a white coffin as it was lowered into the ground. "Blanche was a Bedazzler, and... she liked cats. And knitting. But mostly cats..."

Abby silently thanked God that she'd denied Zane's request to invite the media.

Zane continued. "Blanche died doing what she loved... trying to help a cat, and I guess that's the best any of us can hope for..."

"This is better than I expected," Jack whispered to Abby.

"Yeah, it's not *too* bad."

Zane didn't quit while it wasn't bad. "I, for example, hope I die in bed with a couple of *Zanegirl* cover models. Some people want to be surrounded by family, I guess, but Blanche didn't have a family. She had a cat." He put a hand to his chin. "I'm winging this, and it's getting away from me. The point is: Blanche liked cats."

In these scenarios, people are always looking for words to

repeat. And so a chorus of distant relatives sounded. "Blanche liked cats."

The coffin reached the bottom of the grave, and the crowd didn't hesitate to scatter. In under a minute, the Bedazzlers were the only ones left.

"That went well," Zane said.

"Could have used less talking about sex," Brooks said.

It was the first time Brooks had been able to force himself to visit Staten Island unmedicated in the time Smith had known him, and Smith congratulated him. *Look at you. You're snarking, even.*

"The sentiment was nice," Ana said.

"Yeah," Jack said. "I think."

Doctor Queer's astral form nodded along, but no one saw.

"So, lunch," Zane said. "There's a pizza place with a magma-fired oven I've been meaning to sue for using my likeness. If they're good, I'll let it slide."

"No thanks," Abby said.

"I'm not really in the mood to eat," Ana said.

Brooks scoffed. "If they're not going, I definitely don't like you enough to go."

Zane turned to his last teammate. "Jack?"

Jack shook his head. "I have to go home and feed Butternut and Acorn."

"They're cats," Zane said. "They take care of themselves."

"Yeah, but this is a tough time for Butternut. I want to make sure he handles the transition well."

Everyone shared a judgmental stare at Jack.

"I have nothing to prove here," Jack said, turning to leave.

30

BEDAZZLED

Doctor Queer's mansion was a lot less sad when it was filled with people, and now that it was the new Bedazzlestation, that was the case more often than not. Each team member had their own room, and there was plenty of space to expand the team if they so desired.

They gathered in what Doctor Queer called the Parlour. It was the only part of the house he could reach without floating, at least until Zane Industries employees finished installing the elevator. It was the sort of room that contained scattered ornate, high-back chairs that looked a lot better than they felt. All magical artifacts had been safely stowed, but there was still the enchanted fireplace, aglow with a roaring green flame.[*] Doctor Queer rolled to it and warmed his hands while Abby, Jack, and Brooks gathered nearby to discuss whether it was time to bring in an additional team member.

"Seven is a lucky number," Jack said.

"It wasn't lucky for Blanche," Brooks noted.

"Too soon," Abby said. It hadn't even been three months since their palest teammate's untimely death.

Ana sat as far away from the other Bedazzlers as she could, because she could. Having Blanche's skin grafted onto the

---

[*] Literally. It roared like a lion.

back of her hands meant she had to wear gloves at all times, but that was just fine by her. If she never had to touch another human being's hand again in her life, it would be too soon.

Zane was the last one to arrive at a meeting he'd requested. "I finished reading my biography."

"And?" Abby asked.

"It was about me," Zane said. "I loved it."

Jack turned to Abby. "You quit your job yet?"

Abby sighed. "No. A certain immortal jerk went and released his autobiography the same day my book came out. His is a bestseller, and I can't even break the top thousand."

In the weeks following Blanche's funeral, the public had all but forgotten the kitten rescue. More recently on its mind was an incident in which Zane had tried to break into the Richard Rodgers Theater.

"You're still going to quit your job," Zane said. "You all are."

"We are?" Jack asked.

"Well, not you. You work for me. But you're going to be set." Zane was no longer the team's leader (if he ever was), but he would always be its most forceful speaker. "I called this meeting to talk merchandizing."

"Fantastic," Brooks said dryly.

"Remember the *Monochrome* cartoon?" Zane asked.

Abby tilted her head. "Like on the cereal bowls?"

"Yes. Well. They made a few adjustments, and it's been un-cancelled. Arch?"

The room had been outfitted with a wall of high-definition monitors, a step up from the previous Bedazzlestation. Doctor Queer pressed his remote to turn them on.

"Hot Stuff," Zane said.

The mansion had also been upgraded with the latest Zanehome technology, and Hot Stuff echoed all around them. "What do you need?"

"Roll the tape," Zane said.

On screen was the best that Western animation had to offer. A suave, grey figure ran toward viewers. He was joined by smaller, more distant versions of the other Bedazzlers, and an electric guitar hook signaled the title appearing over them: *Monochrome and Friends*. Heartland rock vocals kicked in moments later:

Monochrome!
Monochrome and Friends!
The greyest guy, always fighting crime
From his tower in the sky
He called some friends to join his crew
And this is how they do:
Agent Brooks is a sourpuss
Always on a different date
Human Touch likes to read your thoughts
And keep you going straight
Torpedo, Torpedo
Valiant and strong
Human Porcupine lives up to his name
He'll get you with his prongs
Doctor Weird is their last teammate
He's Monochrome's oldest friend!
Together, together
Teammates 'til the end!
Monochrome!
Monochrome and Friends!

"I have questions," Jack said.

Abby nodded. "So many questions."

"Kids love a cheesy song," Zane said.

"I don't doubt that, but why am I a giant male robot?" Abby asked.

"Audience testing. Nobody wanted more than one woman

on the team."

"Is that why I'm white and blonde?" Ana asked.

"Bingo," Zane said. "Audiences in the Midwest were uncomfortable with more than one Bedazzler of color, so Jack's the only one."

"I told you I'm not the Human Porcupine," Jack said.

"No, I know. But the kids love animal-themed heroes. Your toy is the most popular after mine."

"And kids love womanizers too?" Brooks asked, referring to his cartoon self, who had his arms roped around different women in each shot.

"Not really," Zane said. "But their parents like it better than a gay character."

"Wow."

"There's already a Doctor Weird," Doctor Queer said. "I don't appreciate my likeness being associated with her name."

Zane held out his hands and motioned for them to settle down. "You guys. It's not a representation of real life. It's a cartoon."

"It's offensive to pretty much all of us," Jack said.

"And what ever happened to diversity?" Abby asked.

"Great idea in New York," Zane said. "Terrible idea for nationwide branding. Urbanites have better things to do than buy toys to fill the hole in their lives."

The Bedazzlers began talking over each other in their antipathy. At least two of them used the word asshole.

"You're each getting fifteen percent of the profits," Zane said.

"That doesn't add up to a hundred," Brooks said. "Let me guess. You're getting more than the rest of us."

"I should, since it's *Monochrome and Friends*. But no. Ten percent is going to Blanche's cat sweater factory."

Abby found that touching, and it made her suspicious. "You said that was a terrible idea."

"It *is* a terrible idea," Zane said, "but apparently there are a lot of Blanches out there who are into it, and they all live in low cost-of-living areas with giant piles of disposable income. I'd be a fool to ignore that market."

"Never change," Abby said.

Zane laughed. "Why would I?"

Suddenly, Zane's voice came from a different direction. "This is an alert. This is a bedazzalert. Get your lazy asses to the Situation Room."

"That's our cue," Abby said. "Bedazzlers... Conve—"

"We're already here," Brooks said.

"I thought we were changing the alert," Ana said.

"We will," Abby said. In reality, she kind of liked the alert.

"Are we married to 'Bedazzlers... Convene'?" Jack asked.

I'm with him, Smith said. *It doesn't really roll off the tongue like 'assemble' or—*

No one paid Jack any attention because Jack was the new Blanche. No one paid Smith any attention because he was still noncorporeal.

Abby stood and repeated, "Bedazzlers... Convene!"

EPILOGUE

Brooks approached Zane Tower for what felt like the ten thousandth time but was actually only the two thousandth. Once again, Zane had lured him in with the promise of a Robotic Body Solution™. The last time Zane promised this, Brooks had walked in on a sad attempt at a pizza party that had four other guests, two of whom were being paid to be there. The time prior to that, Zane had needed cyborg assistance opening a stubborn bottle of kombucha. The time prior to that, Zane had completely forgotten what he'd called Brooks over for. The cyborg had again been forced to use the Q.U.E.E.R. Method to keep from doing something he'd have regretted.

This time was different from the start. Upon entering Zane's office, instead of being presented with an idiotic scenario, Brooks was greeted at the door.

"Come with me," Zane said, roping an arm around him.

Brooks brushed the arm away and offered a suspicious eye. "Where?"

"To the lab," Zane said. There were hundreds of laboratories in Zane Tower, but the trucker was right: saying it with a definite article seemed to give it more weight.

Brooks tried not to get his hopes up. In all likelihood, Zane would take him to the lab to show off a self-pedaling bicycle or an attachment for the NosePhone™. But he could see that Zane's heart rate was up. The billionaire was more excited than usual, which made Brooks excited in turn.

Don't get your hopes up, Smith said.

I know, Brooks said.

As it turned out, getting his hopes up was a safe move.

He entered a lab that looked like a lab, and there, in a glass case in the corner of the room, was Edward Smith. Not the man himself, obviously, but a perfect replica of his original body: 6'0", blond, green-eyed, surly-looking, and complete with not one but two regrettable dragon tattoos, clearly visible despite their risqué placement. That is to say the body wore nothing but a sad pair of briefs.

"Is that what I think it is?" Brooks eyed the motionless body.

"I went with the less chubby version," Zane said. "Figured I'd do you a favor."

It wasn't a favor, but Brooks said nothing.

Zane sensed his displeasure. "If you want, I can fatten him up. He won't be able to fatten himself since this thing can't eat."

Then I don't want it, Smith said.

Brooks ignored his husband. "No, I mean... that's not the kind of robot I imagined. It doesn't look like a robot at all."

"It's not. I told you I'm not interested in robots."

"So it's..."

"It's a sexbot!"

Brooks blinked. "A what now?"

More machine now than man... twisted and evil, Smith said.

You know, once you get in that body I can murder you.

Zane paced and gestured as he explained. "See, with 'robot' you had me thinking little metal factory workers putting widgets together. That bores me. But then I started thinking about all the features your Eddie would need, right? Number one: sexability."

Brooks muttered something in Spanish under his breath.

Zane kept talking. "You are looking at a hyper-realistic simulation of a human body. The skin is just like real skin.

The orifices are—"

"*Oh my God.* Please stop talking."

"I'm screwing with you," Zane said. "It's a clone."

Brooks blinked a few times. "A what now?"

"Well, I tried having my people analyze some of the skin that came loose when I melted your arm, right? They couldn't figure the stuff out. How do you make robots look and feel like people? It's impossible."

"It's not impossible. I exist," Brooks said.

"Well, I have the best people and they couldn't do it, so it's impossible."

Brooks bit his lip. "What did you do?"

"I dug up his body and—"

"*Oh my God.*"

"—cloned him. It was *way* easier than building a humanoid body from scratch."

"Is that even legal?" Brooks asked.

"Would you believe me if I said yes?"

"No," Brooks admitted.

"Well, it is. It's totally legal. We did have to figure out how to age him fifty years to get him to look right, though. That tech's going to be popular with the under twenty-ones..."

I wasn't even forty, Smith complained.

"He wasn't even forty," Brooks said.

Zane rolled his eyes. "Looks right, doesn't he?"

He's got a point, Brooks said.

Smith, aware that he hadn't taken great care of his original body, grumbled, *Yeah. Fine.*

Zane shrugged. "You're going to love it. Literally."

"I'd love it if it were a Roomba at this point," Brooks said.

The consciousness transfer was easy—little more than an *mv* command—and Smith was soon back in as reasonable an approximation of his own body as possible. He prodded his skin a few times, decided it felt right, and moved on with his life. He knocked on the glass container.

"Hey! Let me out of here," Smith said. He pressed his hands against the glass and realized he was confined to about five square feet of pod space. That made him tap (and breathe) harder and faster. "Let me out!"

"Look. He's even got all the same anxieties," Zane said.

"*Great*," Brooks said.

Smith broke into a cold sweat as his knocks became more and more rapid.

"Open the door," Brooks said.

"You people are so needy," Zane said, pressing a button.

The glass door opened outward, and Smith tumbled out. He shook it off and faced Brooks in real life for the first time in nearly a year. For a moment, they stared at each other in total silence. Then the clone rushed the cyborg for a high-concept sci-fi makeout session.

"You're welcome," Zane said to no one as he left the room.

Brooks pulled away to speak, and Smith's mouth trailed his, trying not to let him.

"Eddie," Brooks said.

Smith continued kissing up the side of his neck, taking the shortest possible break to say "What?"

"I missed you," Brooks said, again pulling back so he could look into Smith's eyes.

"I've been here the entire time," Smith said.

"You know what I—" Brooks couldn't finish.

"Oh, no." Smith wiped one of the tears away. "You're going to rust."

"Jesus, Eddie."

Smith pulled him close. "Come on. Let's go home."

Getting home meant passing Godwin Zane in the hallway.

"That was the fastest bang ever," Zane said.

Smith groused. "You'd know."

Brooks shut his eyes. "Gross. Can you just... not mention that ever again?"

"Gladly," Smith said.

"I'll see you at the Bedazzlestation tomorrow, then?" Zane asked.

Brooks opened his eyes so he could give a face of disbelief. "No. No you won't."

"Why not?" Zane asked.

"You shoved my dead husband in my brain and blackmailed me into doing almost a year's worth of favors for you—"

"But—"

"And during that time, you taunted me with fakeout after fakeout to the point that I was ready to have a complete mental breakdown."

"Yeah, but I mean... you're a Bedazzler."

"No. I quit."

"You can't quit."

"I just did," Brooks said.

"But—"

"Find someone else to blackmail."

Zane thought on that. He could, and he would.

ACKNOWLEDGEMENTS

This is my third book, and it's mostly the same people who made this one possible. If you've ever been acknowledged, the acknowledgement still applies. I acknowledge you for life. That means you, beta readers and proof checkers, friends and foes. Jessica Nelson took over editing duties and helped make sure this book wouldn't confuse the hell out of anyone who hadn't read my previous books. For that I am grateful.

Finally, I would like to thank readers both old and new. Heart emoji, heart emoji, face with hearts for eyes emoji. If this book made you smile at all, drop a review on Amazon or Goodreads and help that happy little algorithm find its way.

MORE BY THE AUTHOR

The Brooks & Smith Series:
Time Binge
Time Purge
A Genie Ruins Everything
Fun Times in a Dystopic Hellscape

The Bedazzlers will return in:
The Bedazzlers in Space!

To find out about new releases, join the author's mailing list at martina-fetzer.com, or scan this handy QR code: